the agreement

Three Player Grind Book 2

allyson lindt

acelette press

For my eternal dragon

1
brooke

How MANY PEOPLE in this town would be scandalized if they knew the case I was pulling from the trunk of my car contained two nude angels, intertwined in a passionate celebration?

In my experience, almost as many as were horrified that I'd stayed single for the last fifteen years, since my husband passed. How dare I have raised my twins by myself, rather than finding a man to take care of us?

The gossip used to bother me, but now it was easier to remind myself that people were funny. If they ever realized why this shop was named the way it was—*Deacon's Derelicts and D'Art*—or admitted that they knew, they'd probably die of small-town humiliation.

"*Oh shit. Duck.*" The call was accompanied by the buzz of a small electric motor.

I dropped the case and my head under the hood of the trunk before my brain processed what I was hearing. If I was at Deacon's antique shop and Adam's panicked voice barked an order, it was best to obey first and ask questions later.

A drone slammed into the trunk and clattered to the ground with a pathetic whine, then died.

"Is it safe?" I asked.

"Yes. *Fuck.* Sorry. *Fuck.*" Adam scooped the motorized plane from its resting place. He straightened as I did. "You okay?"

"I'm good."

He ran his hand along the tail end of my partly restored '57 Chevy Bel Air. "And your baby is okay?"

"She's fine. But only because we haven't repainted this sexy behind yet," I teased. "Did your friend survive?" I nodded at his droid.

He shook his head. "I thought I was so close to getting it right this time."

Adam was a modern-day mad scientist. Happy scientist? His current expression of frustration plus bemusement was as close as I ever saw him to angry. "Meh, back to the drawing board. Let me carry that in for you," he said. With dark hair and a square jaw, it would be easy for him to look stern all the time, but instead, there was always a wildness in his eyes and a smile on his lips.

I stepped aside and let him grab the leather briefcase that held my latest restoration project. Muscle rippled under his T-shirt with the stretch. He was a genius-scientist meets romance-novel-cover-model, and I always felt a bit decadent and naughty, watching him work.

That would give the townspeople something to talk about—the forty-year-old widow with two basically adult twins, hooking up with the newcomer to town who was eight years younger.

Not that I'd ever hook up with Adam. Or Deacon. I was older, laden with baggage and kids, and my conservative upbringing still ruled most of my instincts. I didn't mind how frequently Adam cussed, but it wasn't something I could do, and that was just one example.

I'd also only ever been with one man—my late husband. I was pretty sure Adam and Deacon were not only together, no matter how much they denied it, but also both fine with the other seeing other people.

Plus, fantasizing about either of them definitely made for the kind of dreams I'd been told as a child would earn me a one-way ticket to Hell.

We stepped through the front door of the antique shop, and an electric tune greeted us. That was new.

"Addams Family?" I looked at Adam.

"I'm trying out different things. What do you think?"

"How'd the test flight go?" Deacon called from somewhere in the shop before I could answer.

"It was as grand and memorable as the maiden

voyage of The Titanic." Adam led the way, carrying my case further into the store. "But I rescued a damsel in distress from the sinking boat."

We rounded the corner on a row of shelves filled with classic lunchboxes, to find Deacon behind the register. The vase of orange poppies next to him was the only new thing in this place, and I loved the contrast of the fresh flowers with a shop full of antiques.

He looked at me with a smirk. "*Damsel?*"

Deacon was as yummy to look at as Adam, but in a different way. Until about a month ago, his dirty-blond hair had been pulled back into a bun on the top of his head. He'd shaved it all for a charity event, but he swore he'd grow it back. Long sleeves hid arms and a back toned from years of manual labor, as well as some sexy as heck tattoos. He was gorgeous in that I-used-to-be-wild-and-I-still-act-like-it-but-really-I've-settled-down kind of way.

I shrugged. "I was almost taken out by Skynet's grandmother. I'm quite distressed."

"You don't look it." The way Deacon trailed his gaze over me left a wave of heat that would've melted even the most stubborn iceberg, flooding my body.

I hid the reaction under a ridiculous pantomime of wide eyes and holding my hands in front of my face. "Ah. I'm distressed."

"And now you've traumatized my favorite customer. Way to go." Deacon's scowl at Adam was exaggerated.

"What? Chicks dig electric toys," Adam said.

Deacon sighed and rolled his eyes. "We talked about this. Chicks dig toys that vibrate, slide between their legs, and—"

"You need to see what I found." I set my case on the wooden counter with a much heavier *thud* than I needed. If I let him finish that thought, I was likely to turn bright red while my brain shut down. It had taken long enough for me to hear sexually crude language without blushing—I didn't have a problem with it; I just wasn't accustomed to it—but when it came from one of them, my imagination liked to take the words and run.

Even now, I was trying not to fall into the fantasy of Deacon between my legs, showing me tricks my little bullet vibrator never could. I was going to need some me-time when I got home. Rather than fall into that now, I flipped the latches on the briefcase and lifted the lid.

"No shit." Deacon's awe was audible. He grabbed the microfiber cloth I had packed in the case and used it to lift out one of the hand-sculpted, gold-flaked lead figures. My specialty was creating unique figures or restoring old ones. This particular set was an original Brooke. Three characters from The Sandman graphic novels—Dream, Desire, and Destiny.

I started lead sculpting when I was in high school, but it wasn't anything big in my life. I made cute little ladybugs and ribbons because I could. When I lost my husband, I had no idea what I was going to do for money. He'd left us enough to pay off the house and survive for a little while, and I made it stretch, but it wasn't going to last forever.

When a neighbor mentioned they'd been struggling to find a restorer for a hood ornament on their classic Duesenberg but everyone charged a fortune, I asked if I could give it a try. He said he didn't have anything to lose, so he let me at it. The experiment was a success. I realized quickly I could charge a few thousand for a job everyone else wanted ten times as much for.

It was how I met Deacon—I liked to trawl antique shops for items in need of repair and restoration to sell between jobs.

Deacon set the Endless figures tenderly back in their case and frowned. "I can't take them right now. I really wish I could."

"You can take them. They're a gift." I nudged the case closer. "You've been wanting these forever."

"They're gorgeous. I can tell you how much you'll get for them on the open market. They'd be wasted here."

I glared at him. "I'm not concerned about how much they're worth." I let the hurt at his refusal of my gift slip into my reply. "I did the work for you. Not because you asked me to or because I want to be paid, but because it's something you've wanted."

"I'm staying out of this." Adam took a step back.

Deacon scrubbed his face. "They're gorgeous. They really are. And I'm grateful. But"—he pushed out a hiss between his teeth—"I just won't have a place to display them in a month or two."

"What?" My wounded pride vanished, and I stared at him, hoping he didn't mean what I was assuming. "Why not?"

"Someone purchased a lot of the property on Main Street. Big developer. They're going to *revitalize*. I have to update the shop to meet the new design specs set out by the city council, or I'm out."

No. "That can't be right. What about zoning laws and approval? And you own the property."

"Have you ever read Hitchhiker's Guide to the Galaxy?" Adam asked.

What did that— Oh. "Yeah, yeah. *The plans have been on display for months. Locked in the basement.* But that's not actually legal."

"It is, when you have the kind of money these guys do and the lawyers to find the loopholes. The town charter requires me to sell to them if I can't meet building requirements, and they seem determined to give the entire block a more modern look." Deacon shook his head. "Doesn't matter. It's done. I'll deal with the fallout. How are you?"

I wasn't letting him off so easily. I'd answer his question with proof that my random boring life wasn't at stake, and then direct things back to his shop. "You know. Pre-empty nest syndrome, as I watch the twins get ready for their Sweetheart's Dance."

"You need to get yourself a maahhaan." Adam's retort was a poor imitation of a drawl.

I shot him a withering look. I recognized the teasing, but I'd been hearing people say that and mean it for years. The people at church said it first to my face, and then behind my back when I stopped attending. "Thanks. Hadn't had that idea before."

"No. Hang on. He's got a point," Deacon said.

They were not going to shift this conversation to me. Especially not this way.

"Don't even start," I said.

He gave me a look that said, *You know me better than that.* "Hear me out. It's not that you *need a man*, but you need more people to hang out with. Dating is one way."

I hang out here. With you two. But I didn't really. I visited and always made it about work, so I wouldn't have to admit to them or myself that I was here as much for the company and visuals as anything. I didn't have a lot of adult friends. My brother's girlfriend. Her best friend. But they had their own busy lives.

And I hadn't dated at all since my husband passed away. First, I was too grief-stricken, and then, I was raising my kids.

Could Deacon and Adam teach me how to meet a guy? They knew what men their age liked. I didn't want a younger man. Not that the two of them were that much younger, but eight years still seemed like a lot...

And now I was picturing all the yummy things either of them could teach me about relationships. When did I become such a horndog?

"My point is, my life is status quo. Yeah, maybe I'll start dating again—not that I've had any luck so far." Why did I say that?

"How are you not having any luck dating?" Adam's question sounded sincere rather than taunting.

Me and my big mouth. I sighed. "First of all, I'm looking at the town's two most eligible bachelors." *Keep talking before one of them grabs that and runs with it.* "Where am I supposed to meet someone? I'm not a bar person. Or a church person anymore." I still had my faith, but it wasn't attached to the religion I'd grown up in, and I wasn't always on the best of terms with Him. "Dating apps? I had one of those installed for about two weeks. Swiping right... Do you know how many dicks are out there, messaging with inane and trite lines?"

"Enough to make you use the word *dicks* apparently." Adam sounded amused.

He was earning my full supply of withering looks today, but he had a point.

"I'm not surprised every guy wants to know you." There was Deacon again with the kind of boldness I rarely knew how to respond to.

This time, I did. "It's like this for every woman on a dating site. I've had it confirmed."

"Or your friends are almost as hot as you are," Adam said.

My cheeks heated. "Or I'm more of an antique than half the things in this shop, so I look like an easy target."

"*Hey.*" Deacon's voice was sharp. He reached across the counter to loosely grasp my chin and looked me in the eye. "I would put you on any display shelf, but you deserve better. And you are *not* an antique."

The power in his voice stole my thoughts and my breath.

I reluctantly pulled away from his touch. "You can't lose your shop. We have to find a way to save it." I needed this conversation on anything but me, my lack of a love life, and the faint scent of Deacon's cologne mixed with wood and sunshine.

"There's not a way. Adam and I have been brainstorming for days," Deacon said.

"And I'm super creative when it comes to new ideas," Adam added.

He was a brilliant idea guy, but that didn't mean he'd thought of everything.

"You didn't brainstorm with me." Why was I pushing this so hard? Right, because I loved this shop, and Deacon *was* a friend. *A few days* of brainstorming wasn't enough. "I could help you find a solution."

Deacon worked his jaw, and Adam looked between him and me.

"Give me a good reason why the three of us shouldn't at least try." I forced the challenge into my voice.

2

deacon

I DIDN'T WANT to lose my antique store. I loved my little corner of rural-burbia. *Rural-bania? Rural-banalia?*

Besides, the shop had been in the family for generations in one form or another. If I lost it now, I'd never forgive myself.

Brooke was brilliant—and far more stunning than she realized, though that was beside the point—but I had no idea how anyone could get me out of the fact that this shop barely stayed solvent. It wasn't like I could just *try harder* to make enough to comply with the new building codes.

I'd be doing myself, my shop, and Brooke a disservice, if I didn't keep looking for answers and hear her out, though. "Give me at least one good reason why you don't deserve to find a man who loves you for who you are," I said.

What was I doing?

Based on the twin looks of shock staring back at me, Brooke and Adam wondered the same thing.

"Because your shop is an amazing and wonderful thing, and my love life has been non-existent for more than a decade. I don't even know how to date anymore," Brooke said.

Too late to take back what I'd said. If I made light of it, it could be seen as making light of her love life. She deserved adoration and worship, not teasing. "Adam and I do. And if you're helping me figure out how to keep the shop open, it's only fair I offer something in return."

Adam raised his brows, and his thoughts were almost audible. He was asking what the fuck I was doing. Why I didn't just ask Brooke out.

I didn't have to wonder about what Adam's look meant, because it was a conversation we'd had before.

Brooke wasn't my standard hookup. She wasn't a hookup kind of woman at all. She was flowers and dinners and a real courtship and marriage and a family, and she deserved someone who wanted the same.

Regardless of how often I fantasized about handcuffing her to my bed frame and finding out how many ways I could make her scream in pleasure.

How did I know she wasn't interested? Last time I'd cranked up the flirting, she tried to set me up with her brother.

"Me helping you keep your shop open has

13

nothing to do with favors. You don't owe me." Brooke sounded wounded.

That was the last thing I wanted. "And me helping you get back into dating isn't about favors either, but you're looking for something, I'm looking for something…"

"Seems like a reasonable agreement to me." Adam always had my back.

"I'd like your help regardless," I said, "but this lets me do something for you in return."

She chewed her bottom lip, making it look even plumper and rosier. *Fuck*, I wanted to be doing that for her. I'd settle for knowing someone else was.

Brooke's soft smile returned. "All right. It's a deal. But we start with your thing, because it's more time sensitive and has greater consequences if we don't figure it out now."

Hard logic to argue with. "What have you got, idea-wise?" I asked her.

"It depends on what you need to do to your place, to bring it up to the new zoning requirements."

I grabbed the tablet from under the counter that I used for inventory and shop notes, pulled up the research I'd done so far, and slid her the device. "I'd have to update the exterior and make some minor changes to the interior. The facade will be the bulk of the cost. Oh, and the new taxes."

As I talked, I flipped through images Adam had worked up for me, to match the city's new requirements, and finished on a rough estimate.

Brooke sucked on her teeth. "Ouch."

Not encouraging. "Tell me about it."

"Let's start with what you have on hand." She pulled the hair tie off her wrist and used it to tie back her black hair that normally trailed halfway down her back. Perfect length for wrapping around my fist and yanking while I fucked her from behind.

Considering how bright red she turned with light flirting, I was worried she'd walk out and never come back if I got even half as graphic with my words as my imagination wanted me to. I spent a lot more time than I probably should, thinking about the best way to ease her into a more intense conversation. Prodding at her edges and seeing if she was one of those good girls who could go bad. I suspected the answer was *yes*.

That would wait. "I think you've seen everything in the main shop. Most of what's in the back room is there because it either needs work or isn't worth the work." The back half of the building was dedicated to overflow. "What are you looking for?"

"I don't know yet. Right now, I'm wandering to see what comes to mind," Brooke said. "What about the basement? I've never been down there."

I frowned. "I don't have a basement."

She stared back. "Yes, you do."

"I think I'd know if I had a basement."

Brooke held up one finger. "The building has a foundation showing above ground, rather than being on a pad." She held up a second finger. "There's a

Allyson Lindt

hollow sound when you walk across the floor... Okay, so maybe I don't need to count my reasons. There are only two, but they're good ones."

"She makes some valid points," Adam said.

Sure, her logic made perfect sense, with one tiny problem. "I've been through every inch of this shop, and I've never seen a basement entrance. My grandparents never mentioned one. I basically grew up in this place, and I've spent more of my life here than I have in my house. I'd know if there was a basement."

"I swear to you, there's a basement for this building." Brooke extended her hand. "I'd bet on it. Five bucks."

I wanted something tastier. Like Brooke. But not as a wager. Especially since I knew my shop, and I was going to win. "I want one of your pecan pies."

"I'd make you one anyway if you asked."

"That's not the point. You'd give me five bucks if I asked." And I'd do the same for her.

Her smile was bright, confident, and just as gorgeous as flustered-Brooke. "Fair. What do I get when I'm right?"

Adam flipped his gaze between us like he was watching a tennis match. "I say if she's right, she should get first pick of whatever we find down there."

"She's not right, so that's fine with me." This was as much a matter of pride as anything now. I hollered at Dylan to watch the shop and text me if he needed me. "Where do you think this mythical basement entrance will be?" I asked Brooke. My tone was light. We wouldn't find anything, but the view would be good and the company would be better.

Brooke looked around us. "Probably not in the windows."

"Probably not." A shin-to-ceiling wall of glass faced the street.

"No space in the walls between you and the neighbors?"

"Enough for insulation and bricks," Adam said.

Brooke nodded. "Then there's something in the back."

Too easy. But I couldn't pass up the opportunity. "You want to check, Adam?"

"Always." He took a few steps away from the counter and focused on Brooke's behind. "A gorgeous ass that looks even better in good jeans. You're right, Brooke, there is something in back."

Her perturbed look didn't hide her blush or the threatening smile underneath. "Fine. Be boys. If that's what it takes to get you to follow me." She spun, her scowl vanishing into a smirk before she finished her turn, and her ass swaying as she strode away.

Adam and I fell into step beside her. We strode past knickknacks, past the bulk of the main floor where the furniture was on display, and through the door that led to the back portion of the building.

There was about half as much space back here as up front, and it was about twice as full of overflow. Furniture I'd swapped out when they hadn't sold.

17

Fixtures Adam swore could be fixed. Figurines I'd set aside for Brooke. And other random odds and ends I wasn't sure what to do with, but I knew I needed to hold onto.

Despite us all having agreed there was no room in the walls for something like a door or stairs, Brooke headed to the edge of the room first. "The walls are thicker back here." She rapped lightly on the painted brick.

"I didn't say anything." I stood a few feet back with Adam.

She glanced over her shoulder. "You were thinking it. Are you going to help me look?"

"Not part of the bet. But I will teach you the best way to tell a guy he kisses like a fish and show him how to do it right."

Adam snorted. "Lot of practice with that?"

"More than I care to remember."

Brooke rolled her eyes and moved to the next part of the wall.

Teasing her had its moments, but I wasn't enough of an asshole to stand and watch while someone else did the work. I joined her a few feet down, and Adam fell in on her other side.

"I expect you to tell me if you hear something hollow, and not hide it so you can win," Brooke teased.

I grinned. "I'm winning fair and square. Nothing to hide."

Searching the walls didn't take us long, and then

she moved to the rear entrance. There was nothing outside but a blank wall.

"The brick looks different over there." She pointed to an area about six feet wide that came up just a few feet on the building. Not nearly tall enough to be a doorway.

It was weird to say *it's newer*, given that the work was supposedly done almost a century ago, but it was definitely a different size and shape. "My grandpa told me some yahoo got pissed at his grandpa and ran a sledgehammer through it."

"A random dude with a sledgehammer knocked out a perfect rectangle in the original brick?" Adam sounded skeptical.

I frowned. It never occurred to me how weak that sounded, until now.

"Really." Brooke headed inside again and cut as straight a line as was possible through the rows of shelves protruding from the back wall. They weren't built in, but they'd been here for ages and were heavy as fuck to move. Fortunately, I'd never found a reason to do so.

She pressed a finger to her lips. *Shh.*

I wanted to ask if we were hunting wabbits, but she looked so focused, I had to keep my mouth shut. She walked up through the shelves with a heavy step. "I should've worn heels, to get a different echo," she muttered, then looked at me. "Can I borrow a pair?"

"Not sure his shoes are going to fit you," Adam said.

But I knew what she was asking, and I had to admit my curiosity was growing to the point where I almost hoped she was right about the basement. Almost. "Give me a sec."

I headed for the portion of the room with stock I hadn't finished sorting yet, which included a load of vintage clothing I picked up from an estate sale last week. Most of the clothes would go to a friend's shop, in exchange for something nifty she had that she didn't normally deal in, but until then…

I extracted a pair of ruby slippers of all things. They'd be too big for Brooke, but that was better than too small. When I returned and handed her the shoes, she swapped them out quickly for her own sneakers, then resumed her walking pattern.

This time, the echo—or lack of one—was more obvious with each step she took. She paced up and down the shelves, her brow creasing more with each step that sounded the same.

A twinge of disappointment echoed in my chest that she wasn't finding anything, but it was over-written by smugness that I was right.

"Should I grab a pair of shoes and help?" Adam offered.

Brooke shook her head. "It might get hard to hear if there are two of us."

I glared at him.

He shrugged. "What? There could be some neat stuff down there."

"There could be spiders and dirt down there. If there even were a *down there*," I said.

Brooke finished surveying the section near the re-bricked portion of wall and expanded her search. Would she really cover the entire back of the shop? Would that be enough proof? It was pretty much impossible to prove something didn't exist. In this case, I suppose we could start punching holes in the floor, but that wasn't happen—

The sound of her footsteps changed, and we paused.

She tapped the floor again, and then several more times, in a widening square around one corner of a bookshelf. "We need to move this."

"That hasn't been moved… possibly ever." I was approaching it regardless, unable to ignore the bubble of anticipation inside. "How do you want to do this?" I looked at Adam.

He shook his head. "However doesn't get us killed."

"Deal." We angled ourselves, and with a combination of lifting, grunting, and pushing—like sex, but without the orgasm—managed to turn the bookcase sideways.

Holy shit. There was a latch.

3
adam

I FELT LIKE INDIANA JONES.

But without the class of students. Or the boulder chasing me. Or the Nazis.

Unless one or more of those things was behind the large wooden door we'd just lifted, to expose a staircase that vanished into the dark after about five feet.

My frustration over the failed drone flight was gone. A glance at Brooke showed wide-eyed surprise, and when I turned to Deacon, his doubt had shifted to excitement.

"Lamps," I said, I wanted lights that would cover a broader range than flashlights.

"Utility closet. Don't go anywhere, Brooke." Deacon walked toward said closet.

We each grabbed two large utility work-lamps and all but sprinted back to the stairwell.

"Told you so." Brooke had recovered from her shock, but her tone was playful, rather than smug.

Deacon turned on the first lamp and shone it down the stairs. It penetrated the darkness to what might be dirt-packed ground or stone, but not beyond. "If you're lucky, you'll win more than the previously mentioned spiders and dirt."

"Like the Declaration of Independence. *Ooh*, if that's down there, can I have it?" Hey, a guy could pretend, right?

Deacon laughed and took a tentative first step. "Only if Brooke doesn't claim it."

"I'd be too afraid of Nicolas Cage coming after me. You can have it." She followed closely behind Deacon.

I took up the rear. "I'd take him, too."

Deacon glanced back at me. "Dude. Why?"

"I'm weird. Do I need another reaso... *Whoa*." I paused halfway down, as Deacon's light hit the first shapes which looked distinctly like sheets over furniture. Or oddly shaped ghosts. This was way better than figuring out why the drone design I'd 3D-printed didn't fly the way I wanted it to.

We finished our descent into what might as well have been a whole different world. As long as we stayed closer to *National Treasure* than *Cabin in the Woods*, I'd be happy. "We should see how much of the room we can light with the four lamps, and then uncover things."

Deacon set one lamp on the ground near the foot of the stairs. "I'll go east, you go south, and we'll meet at the fourth corner?"

"On it." One of the things I liked about Deacon

was that he understood where I was going with a lot of my ideas, without my having to explain them. Better, he didn't call any of them *nuts* or *too out there*.

Passing so many shapes and not taking a look was killing me. With just a little more luck, the anticipation would pay off. I reached the edge of the light and set my first lamp down. With a right turn, I headed off toward the last corner of the square, and arrived about the same time as Deacon.

His excitement reflected mine. "You still there, Brooke?" His voice echoed off brick walls and stone floors.

"Nope. Ghosts got me. *Ahh*, I'm a zombie now." She had moved to the middle of the light and stood in a circle of sheeted chairs.

Far be it from me to correct someone, but— "Ghosts don't turn people into Zombies."

We joined her.

"I was right about the basement. Do you want to bet me about the ghost-zombies while I'm on a lucky streak?" she asked.

"It's not a streak if you've only done it once, and no. No, I do not." I knew to quit when I was ahead.

Deacon pointed at the nearest pieces. "Pick where you want to start, Ms. I Told You So."

Brooke pointed. "That one."

I had no idea if she'd picked it because it spoke to her, or if that was just the first thing her gaze fell on. I didn't care, as long as there was something weird, cool, or what-the-fuck under the sheet.

Deacon yanked the covering away, and dust clouded the air. "I should've"—he coughed—"thought"—more coughing—"that through."

As the dust settled and the chair became more than a silhouette, my jaw almost dropped.

"It's a pope chair." Brooke hovered her fingers over the purple velvet but didn't make contact.

"A what?" Deacon stared at her.

I was pretty sure no pope ever sat in a chair with wrist straps on the arms and a hole in the seat. At least not that The Vatican would admit.

Brooke pointed at the seat. "Back in the day, there was a woman who tricked everyone into thinking she was a man, and she became pope. Because of that, they made a chair with a hole in the middle, so they could… uh… check a pope's junk."

"I mean, I'm pretty sure you're right about at least half of what the chair is for." I stepped closer and shone the light from my phone on the details. The intricate hand carving was beautiful. It was also a series of stylized people fucking. I gestured for her to come closer, to see.

"I— *Oh*." Brooke stepped back, a flush on her face. "But then, what's it…? Rather, how does it…? I don't…"

Deacon toed a second, smaller piece into view from its spot behind the chair. It could've been an ottoman, but there was a wooden dick sticking out of the middle, and a handle on the side.

I nudged the handle gently with my foot, and as I

turned it like a jack-in-the-box, the dildo bobbed up and down. The mechanics on this thing must be incredible. The toy looked fun too. "Dude, you have a sex chair in your basement that doesn't exist." If it was wrong to be torn between wanting to preserve this piece and wanting to try it out, I didn't want to be right.

I'd been staying with Deacon since I lost my workshop and apartment in a fire two or three months ago, and I loved seeing all the weird things that came through here. But this blew it all out of the water. Even before the sex chair, but especially now. "What else is down here?"

"Let's find out." Deacon turned toward the next shape, but Brooke didn't move. "Are you all right?" When he rested a hand on her arm, she jumped and tore her gaze from the chair.

"I'm fine. Totally. I just... Why are there straps on the arms?"

I swallowed my laugh. She was serious. "Some people like being restrained when they're being fucked."

"Like with handcuffs To the bed. With a partner. I understand that." Brooke was staring at the chair again. "But..."

"The box doesn't work by itself. It's possible there wasn't electricity when it was made," Deacon said.

Brooke continued to stare. The long shadows of the dim light exaggerated the rise and fall of her chest, as her breath came out faster. She looked fascinated, rather than disgusted.

I couldn't fathom being so naive, but I also didn't fault her for it. Since this was an afternoon of wagers, I was willing to bet five bucks Deacon would take this opportunity to hit on her. Again.

Not that I minded watching that back and forth. I wasn't interested in balancing a relationship along with the fucked-up-ness I was dealing with in my head, but I was still male and liked a good show. Their interactions took *slow burn* to a whole new level, and the anticipation was both entertaining and delicious to watch.

Brooke finally tore her gaze away from the seat. "We should see what else is down here. I'm not sure I could find a place for a piece like that in my living room."

My laugh slipped out this time. "Was that a consideration?"

"It is if I get first pick of what's down here." She'd shaken off her fixation.

It was a good thing I'd only bet myself.

Deacon moved on to a longer, shorter sheet-covered piece next. He was more careful unveiling it, which kept the dust to a minimum. The furniture underneath was almost a fainting couch, but the seat flowed up in a gentle curve, instead of being flat. Almost the perfect shape for twisting someone into all sorts of interesting, furniture-assisted fucking positions.

Deacon spent a few minutes examining it, and determined it was probably as old as it looked, and in excellent condition, considering it had been hidden away down here for who knew how long.

We moved on to other pieces, trying to follow some sort of line toward the end of the light. Most of them were like the fainting couch—possibly benign, but possibly with other purposes. Like the benches that weren't the right height, width, or shape for sitting or resting one's feet on.

"We'll be here all night if we keep doing big reveals on these things," Deacon said. "Everybody grab a sheet."

We did. I uncovered a chair. Not a sexy mysterious one with straps or a hole in the middle. As far as I could tell, it was just a wooden chair. It didn't look very comfortable, so maybe if pain was someone's kink…

Which it was for me, and I still wouldn't sit there. Really it was just a chair.

Deacon uncovered a wooden chest. That would be fun to take a peek inside.

But Brooke scored. She was standing in front of a wooden slab almost as tall as her but tilted at an angle. There were definitely straps on this one, and the gear system on the bottom made it look like both angle of board and strap position were adjustable. And there was a hole right about where the face would go if one were leaned against it on their chest.

"Holy shit. It's a Berkley horse." The awe in Deacon's voice matched my excitement.

I didn't know the term. "A what, now?"

"I'm so glad I'm not the only one who doesn't understand," Brooke said.

I was pretty sure I understood the device, just not what Deacon called it.

"Allow me to explain and demonstrate." Deacon reached for Brooke's hand. "Early 1800's, there was this dominatrix named Theresa Berkley who needed a device that made torture more fun."

He coaxed her to lean forward, her face where it belonged.

"So it's not like an ancient massage chair?" Brooke's laugh was nervous, and her voice husky.

"Not quite." Deacon pressed close behind her, to slide his hands along her arms, raising them as he moved. "Wrists are restrained here." He didn't strap her in, but she stayed in position when he pulled away. He wedged her feet apart with his. "Ankles are bound as well, and bottoms come down."

He didn't back away, and she didn't move. Anticipation thickened in the air, as I watched them emit enough sparks to light this entire area. How was this so infuriatingly hot?

"And then the spanking commences." Deacon slapped one of his hands with the other, sending a loud *clap* echoing through the basement.

Brooke's whimper made me instantly hard.

Deacon leaned closer to her until his mouth was near her ear. "And that's how that works."

Was it hot in here, or was it the two of them? Did they remember I was here? Should I say something? Leave quietly and hope Deacon had details later that he was willing to share? Fade quietly into the shadows and see what happened next?

"If you'd like a hands-on demonstration, I can give you one." Deacon's voice was low, with an underlying growl.

Pick me. I wasn't sure if I wanted that or to keep watching.

"I might need—" The opening bars of *7 Rings* filled the room, cutting Brooke off and shattering the mood. "It's Paige." She strained, which sent her straight into Deacon, who caught her with his hands on her hips.

And they were frozen in time again.

Just fuck already.

The song stopped, and the silence was as deafening as the music had been.

"I need to call her back." Brooke stepped away, extracting her phone as she walked

"*Fuck,*" Deacon muttered.

I knew what he meant. "Come back tomorrow with real lighting and finish exploring?"

"Good idea."

"Dude. You have a full-blown actual dungeon in your basement."

Deacon gave a brief shake of his head and turned

to me. "Awesome, right? Think I could introduce her to more of the pieces?"

At least his mind was in the same place as mine. "Signs don't point to *no*."

"I'm sorry. I need to go." Brooke called from the stairs before she scurried up.

"*Fuck*." Deacon slumped back against the Berkley horse. "As long as she comes back tomorrow."

Maybe watching this slow burn wasn't as much fun as I thought.

4

brooke

IT WAS CHILLY OUTSIDE, but the heat from my encounter with Deacon kept me warm from the inside as I drove home to deal with my teenage daughter's latest crisis.

I typically brushed off Deacon's flirting as him being him, but today... I couldn't get how close he'd been out of my head. Was I really going to take him up on his offer for *dating instructions*? It was tempting in a way few things were, even without the details of what he had in mind.

But first, I'd deal with Paige's woes. She'd called me in tears. Their high school Sweethearts' Dance was girl's choice, and a lot of the girls in her school went all out with their *asks*. She preferred not to draw much attention to herself, but she'd put some effort and creativity into the invitation for the guy she wanted to go with.

He'd said *no*.

While she was telling me her story between sobs, I could hear her twin brother, Bryan, in the background. He'd offered to string the guy up for being an idiot.

The two of them were growing up so fast. I swore they were babies just yesterday, and now…

I'd made it clear that they could live at home as long as they needed. There would be no kicking them out at graduation or on their eighteenth birthday, but Paige planned to move out of state and while Bryan wanted to stay here, I doubted he'd be living at home much longer.

The looming empty nest made me both sad and proud. It was also part of the reason I'd decided I could start dating again. I was losing one of my last excuses. Like I'd told Deacon and Adam, though, exploring the whole *dating* thing was daunting. Almost terrifying.

The instant I let myself think of them, the images from the basement rushed back. As did the—*ahem*—unique furniture we'd found.

As I pulled into my driveway, I shrugged off the memories. We lived in a restored farmhouse that had been built around the beginning of the last century. There was an old barn on the back of the lot, and a newer one closer to the house. The new one was where I did my sculpting, and the old one was off-limits.

I'd given the rundown place a glance when we

moved in, more than ten years ago, to find an old tractor under a tarp, and a lot of spiders.

I headed inside through the kitchen door and found Paige sitting at the table, her eyes still puffy and red.

Bryan was holding out an ice-cream sandwich at arm's length. "It's chocolate and sugar. It'll make you feel better."

"I don't want to feel better." Paige's voice was rough. A piece of poster board sat on the table in front of her, with words written in a flowing script, and candy bars stuck in strategic places to provide missing words. The giant card was her *go to the dance with me* invitation. She was halfway through a Snicker's bar, crumpled Sugar Daddy and Uno wrappers discarded next to her elbow.

I took the seat across from her at the table. How was I supposed to tell her this wasn't the end of the world? That she'd find another date, and probably several more, before she finally found *the one*. That wasn't reassuring to someone who'd been turned down by their crush.

I covered her hand. "I'm sorry, hon."

"If you keep eating chocolate, you'll get sick and puke," Bryan said.

She glared at him. "You *just* offered me sugar and chocolate. Besides, maybe I want to puke. The entire cafeteria saw. I'm so freaking humiliated."

"You should puke on his shoes. That'd serve him right." Bryan was in top form this afternoon.

I'd correct him, but the two of them had always had an almost symbiotic bond, and odds were high he was saying exactly what Paige needed to hear, to feel better. "Put the ice-cream sandwich in the freezer or eat it. Your sister already told you *no*."

Bryan shrugged and unwrapped the treat. He shoved the entire thing in his mouth at once.

Boys. I mentally rolled my eyes.

"You're so gross." Paige's words were a sharp contrast to her smile.

"Sure you don't want one?" Bryan asked through a mouth full of chocolate cookie and vanilla ice cream.

Paige made a gagging noise. "*Ugh. So* gross."

"Not as gross as Jason the Idiotic. Please let me go beat him up?"

I wasn't sure they needed me for this, but I did have to do at least a little parenting. "Aggravated assault is a felony, and you're old enough to be tried as an adult. Is he worth the jail time?"

My twins said *no* in unison.

"What do you want to do instead?" I gave them this choice any time they had a problem. "Comfort or solutions?"

Paige slouched in her seat. "I don't know."

Which meant she wasn't receptive to solutions. "Movies and pizza?"

"Can we watch the kind of movies where they fall in love and then one of them dies?" she asked.

Bryan wrinkled his nose. "Dark."

"When your heart gets broken, you can pick the

movie. Go order pizza." I trusted him to get the details right. There were only two pizza places in our small town—a big chain and a local place. We loved the small pizzeria, but they didn't have things like online ordering.

A short while later, we were settled in the living room, first movie up, and pizza on the coffee table between the three of us. Two movies later, Paige was smiling and acting like herself again. She decided she didn't need a date for a stupid dance, and she was going with a friend, to make a statement.

I sent them off to finish their homework before bed, and set to work tidying up the house. Putting dishes in the dishwasher. Sweeping the kitchen floor. As I pushed a chair into its spot under the table, memories of a very different kind of seat flashed in my mind.

The kind we'd discovered in Deacon's hidden basement.

Heat and desire flooded me, pulsing between my legs. It wasn't that I was sex averse. But, I'd only ever been with one man, and for a long time I hadn't been able to imagine being with anyone else. I was open to exploring, but so much of what was out there was overwhelming.

Deacon could teach me.

Except I couldn't picture sex without love, and I knew he was fine with such a thing. I could do sex before marriage, but not a casual *this doesn't mean anything*. I needed a connection. I already had an emotional bond with Deacon. What if something like this afternoon went further, and I took it seriously and he didn't?

I was getting *way* ahead of myself. He'd offered to teach me the ropes of modern dating, not how to screw.

Still, it felt so good to have him pressed against me, his heat at my back, and what I was pretty sure was his erection digging into my behind.

The memory refused to be pushed aside as easily as a few hours ago. It was bedtime, anyway. *Me* time. I had a list of steamy romance books I turned to, when I needed a little extra inspiration. It had taken me years to work up the courage to buy a little vibrator, and even then, it wasn't until I was certain I could order something discreetly online and be the one to pick up the package when it arrived at the house.

I locked my bedroom door, changed into loose clothing, and settled into bed with my eReader. Which book did I want to reread tonight? I was fine with the kissing and slow seduction, as long as it led to the flowery language and the hero's engorged shaft gliding into the heroine's glistening cave.

Nothing caught my eye—none of the old or new titles. Why didn't I have anything with spanking? The sound Deacon made during his history lesson earlier, the *crack* of skin on skin... I swore I could feel that smack on my bare butt.

Carly, a new friend I'd met through my basically sister-in-law, Daria, had given me a list of *gateway* books. She read a lot while she traveled, and she'd said these were titles for when I was ready to be eased into something more intense.

I'd avoided them up until now, not having any idea where to start. This seemed like a good time to find something with spanking in it. I landed on a title Carly said was mostly fun smut with very little plot, and started reading.

The book opened with an open-palmed hand striking a naked ass, and my pulse roared in my ears. I was glued to my screen, as the hero smacked one of the heroine's cheeks and then the other, back and forth, pausing occasionally to dip his fingers between her legs and spread her juices from opening to sex and back again.

Dampness pooled between my thighs. In my head, the hero looked a hell of a lot like Deacon.

Oh my... The people in the story weren't alone. A third person watched. And in my mind, he was Adam.

Was that wicked of me? I'd never pictured real people in place of book characters before, but now I couldn't stop. I was the heroine, bent over Deacon's knee, bare butt in the air and growing redder with each strike.

And the shadowy figure watched us, his arousal obvious as he stroked.

My entire body was lit up like a Christmas tree. I set the book aside and slipped my hand under my panties. My fingers were instantly wet and slick.

I closed my eyes and leaned into my pillow, letting the modified book images play out in my mind. Picturing Deacon paddling then fingering me.

I stroked myself, murmuring silent pleas for an invisible helper to give me more. Push me harder. Begging in a whisper to please let me find release.

Orgasm washed over me, and I shivered under my own touch. I kept teasing until I was spent, and collapsed on the bed with a satisfied sigh.

I held onto the pleasant glow as long as I could, but it slowly slipped away, letting reality back in. Had I just imagined myself with two men? Who I knew?

I understood that people had poly relationships. I was finally wrapping my brain around Colin's. But it wasn't for me, and neither was this raunchy sex. Not in real life.

That didn't mean I had to give up the fantasies or let go of the daydream of Deacon spanking me while Adam watched.

I cleaned up, then sent Carly a text asking for more recommendations like the one I'd just read. Books plus my imagination were more than enough.

I wasn't prepared for anything else.

5
deacon

I WAS AWAKE FAR EARLIER than was sane, if the six followed by other numbers on my clock was to be believed. Not that I'd slept much. My waking mind raced between the discovery in the basement and introducing Brooke to more of it, and when I did fall asleep, the thoughts intensified and became surreal.

The smell of fresh coffee greeted me as I climbed from bed. An upside to having Adam here—he was one of those unholy abominations who thought this was a normal time to be awake. There was almost always coffee waiting when I woke up.

I stumbled into the kitchen, rubbing the sleep from my eyes.

Adam barely glanced up from his tablet and whatever he was doing with the pencil. He liked his thinking time in the mornings, and since I was rarely coherent before eight, I was happy to give it to him.

I grabbed my coffee, black and hot and strong

enough to get me off, and sat down across from him at the kitchen table.

Neither of us talked while I downed the first cup of liquid salvation faster than I should.

"Brandon will be here in about an hour." Adam never looked up from his work, as I went back to the pot for a second cup of coffee.

"Sounds good."

We'd wanted to keep exploring the basement last night, but with only the four lights, it was difficult. Adam's brother knew someone who had a lot of lighting equipment for cameras. Brandon had offered to bring everything over this morning, as long as we were kind to the equipment and let him see what we'd found.

"Put your balls away before then." Adam's delivery was flat, his eyes glued on his screen

I looked down and snorted in disbelief at the sight of my dick hanging out of my boxers. The coffee might need to be stronger. "Fine. I guess." My sigh was exaggerated. I adjusted myself and leaned against the nearby counter.

"Should I be grateful you weren't dreaming about Brooke?" Adam finally gave me his attention.

I quirked my lips. "Or disappointed you didn't get to see the results."

Adam and I met online a few years ago, when his then-girlfriend decided she wanted a threesome. He and I hit it off, but she was disappointed her bisexual boyfriend was making out with another man as much as he was with her.

That night soured their relationship, and a few months later, when his father passed away, she decided she didn't want to deal with his grief.

He was better off without her in his life.

Adam and I had stayed good friends, with occasional benefits, but we made far better friends than anything else. Neither one of us was the long-term-romance kind of guy.

He was the ultimate wingman, though.

"I'm disappointed I didn't get to see the results last night," Adam teased.

"You and me both."

"Do you want me to say it?"

To tell me, *again*, that I either needed to make a move for her or away from her? "No."

He shrugged.

"Brooke's not the kind of person either of us usually hooks up with. You heard her yesterday—modern dating is a little weird—plus you saw how bright red she got with that chair. With anything sexual."

"Which you rarely fail to exploit."

I stared at Adam. "Your point is?"

"It's a bit elementary school. If you want to pull the pretty girl's pigtails to tell her you like her, maybe follow it up by asking if you can fuck her at the same time."

I sank in my chair and let out a long breath. "I

know." I couldn't say why I kept fixating on Brooke. The challenge? Maybe. Or because she was different. Sweet. Smart. Sassy.

"Shit or get off the pot," Adam said.

I wrinkled my nose. "You couldn't have used a better phrase when it comes to sex?"

"I probably could've. Your reaction wouldn't have been as fun." He grinned and pushed back from the table. "I'm heading downstairs, to make sure we're set for Brandon. Come find me when you have pants on."

I hated to admit that Adam was right, mostly because that meant admitting I was wrong, but what was I doing with Brooke? Last night, pressed close to her back, hearing the soft whimpers and sighs she made with me barely touching her, and I'd been rock hard.

But a woman like Brooke wanted—deserved —*long term*. Only one partner. Ever? I couldn't fathom. Pursuing my attraction to her would be about lust for me, and when it ended, I guaranteed she wouldn't want to stay friends, the way Adam had.

So, no. I might keep flirting, I was who I was, and I'd definitely help her navigate the dating world if she was serious about taking me up on my offer, but I wouldn't sleep with her. No matter how tempting the idea was.

I shook aside the thoughts, showered, and dressed so I could head downstairs.

Brandon was here, unloading lights from his SUV

with Adam's help. Watching them together over the last few months had been uncomfortable. When the fire happened at Adam's, he originally went to his brother's, but their relationship was already fragile, and a blow-out of a fight had broken a fractured bond.

Apologies had been made, and the two were working to repair years of pain, but frequently they didn't say much when they were in the same space. Like now. It was still better than when they refused to see each other, though. That had hurt Adam more than he'd admitted.

As soon as Adam saw me, he grinned. "I thought you'd like to be here for any sharing or big reveals."

"It's more furniture, isn't it?" Brandon asked. "How big a reveal is it?"

I pointed to two boxes of lights and grabbed a couple of portable screens. "Follow me and decide for yourself." We trooped down the stairs, and I set my load aside and turned on the closest lamp we left down last night.

"Is that..." Brandon stared at the seatless chair, mouth slightly open.

"A *pope chair*." Adam repeated Brooke's response, a hint of amusement in his voice.

Brandon turned his stunned look on his brother. "You can't actually think that."

"He doesn't." I laughed. "We've only uncovered a few pieces so far, but..." I walked toward the next stopping point, shining a light on the various benches. I'd done a bit of research last night, in between fits of trying and failing to sleep, and confirmed that these were used for bending people over in various positions.

"*Fuck me*," Brandon muttered.

I snorted. "Pretty sure that was the point, yes."

He shook his head. "I need one of these. Talk about an amazing Valentine's Day gift."

"I don't want to hear about that." Adam stuck his fingers in his ears. "La, la, la, la, la."

Brandon rolled his eyes. "Like you're so sweet and innocent."

"I'm not. But that doesn't mean I want to picture you using one of those benches."

"I wouldn't be the one *on* it," Brandon said.

"*La la la la la*," Adam sang louder.

Absolutely ridiculous. Maybe these two were getting along better than I'd realized. "I need to make sure none of them are part of a set, but you're welcome to one if you want it," I told Brandon.

"Perfect. I'll pick it up with the lights."

I didn't expect him to ask for a price or let me give him one of the benches. He insisted I treat him like any paying customer, and he had a bigger budget than I did. But I would knock off something for him bringing us the lights, and just not mention it.

Once his SUV was unloaded, Brandon had to run, to make an appointment. Adam and I spent the rest of the morning setting up enough lights to get a good view of the entire basement. The space was larger than my shop, extending under Aubrey's clothing shop next door.

With more light, Adam started recording as we uncovered and sifted through everything else. The furniture down here wasn't tightly packed into the space. In fact, depending on how we positioned things, it was about enough to furnish this basement.

And most of it was similar to what we'd already found—benches, chaises, wicked chairs, bed frames, and a few sets of stocks—long wooden boards with holes in them for heads and wrists, meant to restrain and publicly humiliate.

Realization tickled my thoughts, but my brain was snagged on the refusal to put all these pieces into the picture they made.

Against the far wall, we found a series of silk privacy screens with delicate, gorgeous, and blatantly pornographic artwork on them. There were several chests and wooden wardrobes next to the screens, as well. Inside, we found corsets, garters, ruffled skirts, and high heels.

Aubrey was going to love this shit.

And I was picturing Brooke in the white corset with red trim, and nothing underneath it, maybe strapped to one of the crosses—

"Dude, I think there was a sex dungeon in your basement." Adam's comment forced me to admit what I'd been trying to ignore since we came down here.

Because— "My family built this place. My great-times-four grandfather and grandmother. No one else has owned it but my family." And if Adam didn't want to admit his brother had sex, I *really* didn't want to imagine my grandparents holding paid orgies in their basement. Besides, no one had ever mentioned it. Not my family, not the history books. I'd never even heard rumors. "I'd know if there used to be a secret brothel down here."

"Would you?" There was a challenge in Adam's retort. "Because yesterday you didn't even know you had a basement."

He had a good point.

6
adam

THIS PLACE WAS SO MUCH BETTER than a cave with a gilded egg or the Arc of the Covenant or the Holy Grail.

Maybe not that last one. Eternal life would be a lot of fun, especially with access to all this equipment.

Deacon and I spent several hours cataloging, with him making notes and me taking pictures and video. When I lost my workshop late last year, I'd lost a part of me as well. Nothing in there had been irreplaceable, for the right price, but the venture had felt like *the* idea. The one I could stick to. The one that would finally give me direction.

I still had a lot of ideas—it was who I was—but none of them grabbed me now.

Since last night, that inspiration was back. Sure, this was Deacon's stuff, his find, but it sent my imagination racing over the possibilities. Were exploration-heist-porn movies a thing? No, *porn* was the wrong word for it, because I wanted this movie to have a plot but also have scorching sex.

Like that movie with Deadpool and Black Adam and Wonder Woman, but they all fuck at the end. And in the middle. And the beginning—

"Anyone home?" Aubrey's voice carried through the room.

"Back here," Deacon called.

I raised my brows. "*Back here* is not a direction."

"No, but I can follow the sound of your voices." Aubrey joined us.

"Unless there are echoes and ghosts, trying to misdirect you."

She looked at me with her mouth twisted, and poked me in the arm. "You don't feel like a ghost."

"I've taken a corporeal form, specifically to haunt this realm." I liked Aubrey. She and Deacon had been friends since they were kids, and she usually had a similar sense of humor to his.

They were more like siblings than friends, with the frequent friendly spats and zero sexual tension between them. Aubrey might as well be Deacon's sister.

She rolled her eyes. "You're such a dork. A vampire would've made far more sense and taken fewer mental acrobatics to justify."

"A vampire who hid in a basement for more than a hundred and fifty years and never fed?" Deacon's question was heavy with disbelief.

"Uh… *yeah*. He was hibernating. Or mourning, like Lesta— Are we under my shop?"

Deacon looked at her and then up. "Pretty sure."

"*Wow*. I came over to pick up that box of clothes, and Dylan said you'd found a door. I had to come see for myself, but this is way cooler than I expected." As she talked, she cast her gaze around the room. "Holy… Are those…?"

"Corsets and skirts and stuff," I said to her retreating back.

We followed her to one of the open trunks.

"*And stuff…*" The fact that she was muttering didn't hide her disgust at his phrasing. She held up one of the corsets. "Handmade. Real silk. Actual boning—"

My snicker slipped out, and she glared at me.

"Not that kind of boning," she said.

Deacon snorted. "He knows. And you said it again."

"*Boys.*" She grabbed the flashlight Deacon was carrying and shone it on the details of the clothing. "This is fucking incredible. You're going to let me put these up on consignment for you, right?"

"As soon as Brooke has a chance to look at it all," Deacon said.

Aubrey's irritation and disbelief turned genuine, all traces of humor vanishing, but her half-smirk returned so fast I must have imagined otherwise. "Is she going to encase one of them in lead? Because I hate to be the one to tell you this, but Brooke's expertise is not vintage clothing."

"She bet me I had a basement, and I was sure she was wrong. As you can see..." Deacon swept an arm around the room. "She gets to pick from what we find."

"I suppose that's fair. As soon as you're ready, I'll help you price the clothing out and put it on display." Aubrey glided her hand over a skirt, never making contact.

Footsteps echoed on the stairs, like work boots on wood, and Brooke's *hello* reached us.

"I need to get back to work." Aubrey stepped away. "Let me know on the stuff."

"I thought it wasn't *stuff*," Deacon called as she strolled away.

She flipped him off over her shoulder.

Yup. Total siblings.

Brooke turned to watch her leave, then joined us. "Was it something I said?"

The question struck me as odd for reasons I couldn't quite place. "She had things to do."

"I was worried you might not be back after everything we found yesterday." Deacon's tone was light and playful, but I heard the seriousness underneath. Did he have any idea how bad he had it for her?

And how did she not?

"I would've been here sooner, to see what else you found, but Mom life called," Brooke said. "Impressive haul. Laura Croft would be envious."

That was what I was talking about.

"Oh, *wow*." Brooke wandered past us and stopped in front of one of the wardrobes. The way she tilted her head, rather than opening the doors, she probably wasn't looking to see if it went to Narnia.

Sexy, explicit Narnia. *Fillory.*

"Those are amazing." She pointed to the decoration on the top.

I shone a light up to get a better look. It was an intricately detailed arch. "It's people fucking."

Pink colored Brooke's cheeks. "But the design work is incredible."

"I won't argue that," Deacon said. "Do you want to look around at everything before you pick your prize, or have you already seen what you want?" His tone slid down half an octave.

Brooke glanced at us, bottom lip caught between her teeth, then turned away. "I'm not taking anything."

"But you won. Do you have any idea how hard it is for me to admit I was wrong?" Deacon asked.

She shook her head. "We went looking because we're trying to save your business. I can't take away from what may be the solution. No arguments."

"Did you just use your *Mom voice* on us?" I laughed.

Brooke pursed her lips. "Never." She almost sounded offended. "But I will help Deacon restore anything like that"—she nodded at the arch—"that you find down here."

"Do you want any more explanations of positions or furniture use to go with your work?" Deacon asked.

"It might be helpful. I need to make sure my restorations do the originals justice."

Frustration surged in from nowhere. I wasn't in the mood to watch the verbal version of blue balls tonight. Which was weird—it never bothered me before. Maybe if I fucked off to do my own thing, these two would get their fuck on already.

After all, there was a sex dungeon in Deacon's basement, so weirder things had happened.

No. Never mind. Deacon and Brooke finally moving past this, whatever it was, was weirder than secret underground fuck-benches.

"I'm going to go edit this video and turn it into something," I said. "Several somethings. You're cool with me uploading all of it?"

Deacon nodded. "Mention the shop if you can."

"Always." I'd be hurt he thought he had to ask, but given the way he was looking at Brooke, this wasn't about me, anyway.

I left the two of them to do what they weren't going to do, and headed back upstairs. Ideas spilled through my mind about the best way to spin this find. I had a YouTube channel that changed focus as often as my brain did. Not a lot of subscribers, but I had fun making the videos.

The contents of Deacon's basement could be an entire series, though.

A giggle drifted up from below, and I cringed. Why was this rubbing me so wrong?

I should've filmed the search for the hidden trap door yesterday, but I could at least get shots of everywhere we looked. I wandered through the back of Deacon's shop, filming the same path we'd followed when we were exploring. The series could focus on aspects of the journey, mixed with the different types of things we'd uncovered, and finish by pointing people to Deacon's and Aubrey's places, since she'd have the clothing we found.

It was awfully quiet down there. Which it should be. I wasn't close enough to hear the conversation, and there was absolutely no reason for me to holler *everything okay?*

Nope. I was going to work on my videos, revel in the excitement of this discovery, and get over this bothered feeling about the exchange between Deacon and Brooke this afternoon.

7

brooke

DESPITE MY QUALITY alone-time last night, thoughts of Deacon's place hadn't left me alone all day. Of what we'd found in his basement and that he seemed to know exactly what it was all for and how to use it.

We spent a few hours going through everything he and Adam had uncovered, and I made mental notes about what I could do restoration on, what I could add new details to, replace pieces of, and more. And every other piece, Deacon had a comment about purpose, or demonstrations of use, or something equally enticing that had my pulse hammering in my ears.

I reached a point where my skin wasn't cooling and the throb between my thighs was impossible to ignore. I was used to a direct, teasing Deacon, but this was a whole new level of temptingly explicit.

"How do you do it?" My question slipped out before I could decipher what I meant.

He looked at me, puzzled. "Do what?"

"Treat sex like it's no big deal." That wasn't quite what I wanted to know, but it was close.

"You misunderstand."

"Help me get it, then."

Deacon grasped my fingertips and pulled me toward some normal chairs on the other end of the basement from the stairs. He nudged me into one and sat across from me. "It's not that it's no big deal, but when you take the emotional attachment out of it, sex can be really incredible or just plain funny. Think about it. It's sticky. It's messy. People do the most ridiculous things to get it."

I'd never thought about any of that. To me, sex was this thing people in love did that felt good. "I am so screwed when it comes to dating. But not, because I don't get any of this. I feel like a freaking forty-year-old virgin."

"My experiences are different than yours—it doesn't make yours bad, only different. You're in a small town in Utah, and you're far more likely to find people with your experiences than mine. You can find "

"A nice Mormon divorcé or widower who's only ever been with one woman and wants me to be his second wife, so he can parade me in front of the congregation?" *No, thank you.* "Would you want that?"

"I see your point." Deacon smiled through his scowl. "Though if said widower were parading me in front of the other people at church, I'd be highly amused." And there he went, making a joke of things again.

"It's not that I want to go out and screw around, but there has to be a middle ground between celibacy and doing everyone." Did I imply... "Not that you are. I didn't mean that."

Deacon didn't look bothered. "There is a middle ground. You just have to find it."

"How?" Why was I pursuing this conversation here and now? Because letting the questions bounce in my head wasn't helping, and he wasn't shutting me down. And part of me wanted to see what kind of *lessons* he could give me. A large part of me. "Can people really enjoy sex without being emotionally attached?" I asked.

His eyes grew wide, reflecting my surprise at what I'd said aloud.

"Adam and I do," he said.

"But you're together." They had to be. They were so close.

"No. Rather, we're friends, but we're not more."

I didn't get this at all, but I wanted to. "That means, when there's sex, there's emotional attachment, because you're friends. How do you keep the line from blurring? I don't want to be the woman who throws all reason to the wind because a guy is a good kisser." I was really baring my soul today. How did Deacon bring that out in me?

"If you don't want that, don't be that woman."

I gave him a withering look. "Like it's that simple."

Deacon huffed a sigh. "I realize it's not, but the theory is solid. What I'm going to tell you next will sound deceptively simple but complex at the same time. If you don't want to confuse an emotional relationship with a physical one, look at the two separately."

"This was a mistake." I was an idiot for thinking I could talk to him about this.

When I stood to leave, he grabbed my wrist and a fresh shock of heat spilled through me.

"I'm not done." His voice was as firm as his grip, and he stood to look me in the eye.

I swallowed past my suddenly dry throat. "Okay...?"

"What you and I are doing right now—is it romantic?"

Was it? I knew better. It was turning me on more than I expected, though. "No."

Deacon rested a hand on my cheek, scorching my skin. "Focus on my touch." His voice was low and even, sliding over me like satin. "Don't think about what your heart is saying but pay attention to how your body feels."

"Okay." Like I had a choice but to listen to my body. My racing heart. The anticipation coiled in my belly. The way my breath wanted to tear from my chest in short pants. "I think I get it." My voice wavered.

One corner of his mouth tugged up. "You sure?"

Not even close. If he hadn't led with the whole *don't think about your heart*, I'd be tumbling into a myriad of questions about whether this meant anything. That didn't mean I wanted him to stop. "I might need a little more explanation and practice."

"As you wish." Deacon brushed his lips lightly over mine, and the rest of the world fell away. He glided his mouth along my jaw, up to my ear. "See? Just the physical." His hot breath teased my skin with the whisper.

I wanted to whimper. This was just a kiss. It didn't mean more. I repeated the words in my head while the faint tingle of his lips lingered everywhere he'd kissed. "I think I get it." In theory, I did. In practice, maybe not, because I wanted him to keep going.

"You're sure?" Deacon pulled back to search my face, but didn't drop his hand. "You don't want more practice?"

I so very much did. "Like what?" My question came out breathy.

"You want to be prepared for anything dating throws your way. If the opportunity comes up, you want to seize it, don't you?"

As opposed to holding back out of terror or lack of experience? "Yes." I wasn't going to become someone else when it came to certain behaviors, but I'd hate to miss out on a great guy because sex terrified me.

"In that case..." Deacon trailed a finger down the middle of my chest, stopping to tug on my waistband

and pull me closer. "How about a full-on, hands-on lesson?"

"Yes, please." I didn't mean to say that out loud.

Deacon's deep chuckle told me it was the right answer. He nipped at my earlobe and kissed along the shell of my ear. "You just have to remember two things," he whispered. "This is about the physical, not about love. And if you're not enjoying it, you tell me to stop. Can you do that?"

I nodded, unable to find my voice.

He dragged his thumb over my bottom lip. "Good girl."

I practically melted into a puddle at his feet.

Deacon dropped his hands to my hips and guided me backwards until my calves hit something. He lowered me onto one of the fainting couches and sat facing me.

We were still in his basement. The shop was probably closed by now, but Adam was likely around.

"What if someone walks in on us?" I asked.

"They won't." He rested a palm on my waist, under my shirt.

"But what if they do?"

He glided his palm to my stomach and inched higher. "They can watch."

Holy heck, why did that make me slick with anticipation?

"Unless you want to stop." Deacon's touch stalled.

I doubted Adam would come looking for us, but

the idea of him, standing in the shadows watching… *Oh my*. "No. I don't want to stop."

Deacon's hot, calloused palm against my skin was a new kind of anticipation, as he kept his touch to my stomach and breastbone. He crushed his mouth to mine with a hard abandon that hadn't been there before, and I kissed back. Our tongues tangled in a frantic dance. How was he making me feel this good with such simple sensations?

Deacon glided his lips down my neck, pausing to suck on the skin, before traveling lower to nip at my collarbone.

This was like in the books I read, but so much better and a lot more explicit in real life. I wanted to touch back, but I wasn't sure where or how. I ran my fingertips tentatively along his inner thigh, up to the distinct bulge, and lightly traced the outline of his erection.

He sucked a sharp breath through his teeth and let out a groan that was as yummy as his touch. "What are you doing?" His voice was raw.

"This can't be one-sided. I want to touch too."

His hands fell away from me in a blink, but he grabbed my wrists before I could register disappointment. The way his fingers dug into me made me think of a barely controlled beast.

Hot.

"I'd hate to overload you with instructions." His tone was still low and measured.

I was already on overload. "I have to learn, eventually."

"You can't shove everything into your brain at once. Save some of it for the next lesson."

"You assume there's going to be a Lesson Two." I suspected my teasing was playing with fire, but I couldn't help myself.

He smirked. "There's a lot to learn. This is more than just sex."

"But the point is that it is *just sex*."

"Exactly."

"So confusing," I said playfully. "Make me want a Lesson Two."

His grin was as threatening and enticing as his growl. "You will."

"What are you going to do if I touch you anyway?" I couldn't help it. This was fun.

"I'll restrain you."

I liked the sound of that. What had he unleashed in me? I twisted free of Deacon's grip and dragged a finger down his chest.

He snatched a silk scarf from the top of a nearby clothing pile, wrapped it around my wrists, and pinned them above my head. I tilted to watch him tie me to a chair that was butted against the couch behind me. "Resourceful."

"You have no idea." He was rough when he shoved my shirt up, as if he'd shed a veneer of calm. The elastic from my bra left a burn in its wake when he shoved it out of the way.

My heart was in my throat. Was I really doing this? Decades of expectation and indoctrination and other people's opinions surged in around me.

Deacon pulled away to look me in the eye. "Are you all right?"

I wanted to do this with someone, to adapt and adjust and figure out how it worked, and I couldn't think of anyone better than him. "Yes."

"Good." His grin had returned. He dipped his head and wrapped his lips around one of my nipples. As he licked and sucked, he kneaded the other. The intensity made my head swim, and he kept the attention up until I was squirming underneath him.

Could I get off this way? Because I swore I was close.

Deacon moved his mouth back to mine. "Still staying removed? Focused on how your body feels?"

I couldn't think about anything *but* how my body felt. "Yes."

"Good." He swallowed my moan with another series of kisses, as he glided a hand down to undo my jeans. He slipped under my panties.

I gasped when he slid between my legs, along my slick skin. It felt so very different to have his hands down there than my own. His fingers were pressed tight against my skin, sandwiched between me and my clothing, but somehow he managed to slip them inside me.

I bucked into the penetration, thrusting against his

hand as he pumped. When he withdrew, he moved up to the throbbing button I knew would get me off.

Deacon teased until I was panting. Nothing existed except us, in this moment. Climax built inside, and when it washed over me, I had to bite my cheek to keep from crying out.

He eased his touch away as I shuddered with pleasure, then flicked his tongue over his glistening fingers.

My heart hammered at the sight. I'd never... "What do I taste like?"

"Find out for yourself." He leaned forward and pressed his fingers to my lips. And then he was kissing me and licking me from his skin and letting me lick him clean.

This was incredible.

When he straightened and said, "I'm going to get something to clean you up with. Don't move," I was surprised.

"We're not done," I said.

"You enjoyed yourself, didn't you?"

"But you didn't..."

"I promise you, I did. Besides, Lesson Two."

As soon as my brain power returned, I'd be daydreaming about what that involved.

8

deacon

I DIDN'T WANT to send Brooke home, but the compulsion to keep her here, to fuck her all night and into the morning felt dangerous. With her lack of experience, I needed to find that line between tasting her and making sure I didn't destroy our friendship. Ensuring I didn't hurt her.

When I got up in the morning, I grabbed my phone. There was a text from Aubrey that read, *What did you do?*

No way was she talking about Brooke and me. *What are you talking about?* I sent back.

When the message sat on *Unread* for more than a few seconds, I got tired of waiting for an answer.

I wandered into the bathroom and stripped out of my clothes. My half-hard cock gave a half-hearted salute. I was pretty sure the poor guy had been in this state most of the night. What would've happened if I hadn't stopped with Brooke? Stripped her out of her clothes, slid inside her, and taken her while she was bound to that couch?

And now I was fully erect. I scrubbed my face and stepped under still-cold water in the shower. The icy spray was a shock to my system, but it didn't clear out the teasing thoughts.

My imagination picked up where I'd left off with Brooke. Instead of me sending her home after the orgasm, her clothes came off and so did mine.

I fisted my cock as I pictured myself buried inside her, and in my fantasy, Adam emerged from the shadows.

This was nice. Especially since he had his dick out.

It was easy to lose myself in imagining how good Brooke felt wrapped around me. Of being watched. This time, when Brooke came, she was loud. She let out an incredible scream of pleasure that rocketed through me and tugged at my mounting need.

One of the incredible things about a fantasy was no condoms required. I spilled inside her, pumping until I was spent.

When imaginary-Adam approached, I slid to the floor on my knees and took him in my mouth, sucking until he finished in my mouth.

In real life, need tightened in my balls, pressure building with anticipation. My legs wobbled when I came. A sticky mess splashed on the wall and coated my hand, and I kept pumping until it was too much.

I needed either Brooke or Adam here. Or both.

Or neither. Last night was just sex. Hell, it wasn't

even that. It was an orgasm for Brooke, and if my hand was good enough for her, it worked for me too. And the next time wouldn't mean any more than the last time.

I finished my shower and dressed with a tuneless song bouncing in my thoughts.

Adam wasn't in the kitchen. Or his bedroom. Not surprising, given his excitement for the discovery, and the fact that it was after nine.

The nameless song looped in my head, and I hummed to myself as I headed downstairs. Adam's voice drifted toward me as I walked toward the shop, and mingled with the fantasy from the shower. How many lessons, until Brooke was comfortable letting him join us?

How many lessons would there be, total? Should I put a cap on things? *No more orgasms after Lesson Five?* Five definitely felt low.

Brooke's laugh reached my ears, mingled with Adam's, and a weird spike jabbed my chest. I shoved it aside and joined the two of them in the main shop. "Morning."

The flush that spread across Brooke's face and her soft smile held a whole new meaning this morning.

"Dude, you need to check the store's voicemail." Adam jerked his head toward the front door. "And look."

Huh? I followed his nod, to see five people waiting outside the shop, none of them familiar. We didn't open for half an hour, and the lights were still off in here, but that didn't stop one of the visitors from pressing his hands and face to the glass and peering inside.

"What's going on?" I asked.

"Messages first," Adam said.

This was getting weird. It was a rare day that we had one message, and this morning there were five. All of them asking about specific pieces of the new furniture.

I was listening to the last one, when Aubrey called my cell. I answered. "What's up?"

"I have people calling me, asking about *the dresses in the video*. What video?"

I looked at Adam, who was watching me with a self-satisfied expression, and put Aubrey on speaker so she could hear me ask him, "What video?"

"I posted a teaser online, last night, of what we talked about. Highlights of the stuff we found, with a note that said a full series was coming soon. I woke up to over two-hundred thousand views." Adam grinned.

"You didn't tell me that. Congratulations." Brooke's enthusiasm was palpable.

And alluring. What would it take to make her this kind of excited more often?

Adam's smile grew. "I wanted to tell everyone at once. It killed me to sit on that. You need to wake up earlier, dude."

"She's right—that's amazing," Aubrey said. "But what am I supposed to tell these people who are calling me? One said she was driving in from Ely and hoped I still had something to see when she got here."

Ely Nevada was more than six hours away. —*the fuck?* This was awesome publicity, but there was no way I was set up to receive the business. "I can't let people wander around that basement. It's barely safe for us." And I didn't have the room to bring so many pieces up here. "What did you show in the preview?"

Adam sent Aubrey the link, and she said she'd be over as soon as she'd watched it and processed. Then he pulled the video up for us. The three of us huddled around his phone was cozy, but there were other things to focus on.

Fortunately, the short video only highlighted a few pieces. When Aubrey showed up, coming in through the rear entrance to avoid the small crowd, we had twenty minutes until we both opened our doors. I pointed to her and Brooke. "You two carry the applicable clothing over to Aubrey's. Adam and I will haul up the furniture in question."

Brooke gave a lazy salute. "Yes sir."

I did like the way she said that.

Carrying the heavier pieces up the stairs was rough—I had no idea how they'd gotten down there in the first place—but finding a spot for them on the sales floor was almost as difficult.

Brooke came back and insisted on helping with the furniture. Which was good, since we barely finished as it was time to open the shop.

The five people waiting turned out to be two

couples, and one individual who took a quick look at what was available and said he'd be back when I had more ready to view.

"Leave your email, and we'll let you know when the rest is coming up," Brooke said. "We promise we only email when there's furniture news."

Smart thinking. I didn't have anything like a newsletter, but apparently, I was about to.

The guy left his information, and the two couples wanted to sign-up as well.

"Feel free to take your time looking around," I told them.

"We'd like the set of four high-backed chairs," Michael said.

Brooke was definitely brilliant for getting their contact info.

Mr. Johnson—he and his wife hadn't given their first names—held up a hand. "We'll give you eight hundred for the set."

Which was less than I'd charge, but more than I was willing to negotiate down to.

"One grand," Michael countered.

Mr. Johnson frowned. "I can go to eleven hundred."

What was happening? The chairs were neat and well preserved, but without an incredible restoration, they weren't worth much. If either of these couples wanted to restore and resell, they'd struggle to find the right buyer.

Unless I'd been wrong in my appraisal. Which I never was.

"Fifteen hundred." Michael really wanted these chairs.

Mrs. Johnson scowled. "They're not worth it."

"Aren't they?"

Was there an actual bidding war going on in my shop? Maybe one of those wardrobes really did transport us to a magical world.

Mr. Johnson shook his head. "Can't go that high, but make sure you let me know when the rest is ready to look at," he said to me.

"We will." Brooke was warm and friendly, as she shook his hand.

As Adam and I helped load the purchase into the back of a pickup, I was spinning ahead to the next steps. I had an idea what to charge for most of what we'd found, though some would need more research.

That didn't mean I had a place to put them.

We sent Michael and his wife, Veronica on their way. There was a text waiting for me from Aubrey, saying she'd sold two of the dresses.

"You'll need to make the basement part of your showroom," Adam said as we rejoined Brooke.

Saying it didn't make it any more plausible. "The place is lit with borrowed lights. There's no power. The stairs need to be looked at more closely. It's a great idea, but there's no way."

"I can wire you for electricity." Brooke made it sound like it was nothing.

I appreciated the offer. "If I do that, it's going to have to be code. Work done by licensed people."

"I am." She scrunched up her face. "Rather, I was. It may have lapsed, but it's easy enough to renew the license."

"Since when are you licensed?" And why didn't I know that?

She shrugged. "I found myself doing a lot of rewiring to support the sculpting and welding, and it was cheaper to learn to do it myself and get licensed, than to keep paying an electrician to come out."

"And I can take care of the stairs, plus block out enough of the walls and flooring to bring it up to code without damaging the original structure." Adam had worked for a contractor a few years ago, when he wanted to build the houses he'd designed.

Their offers were fantastic, but I couldn't take them up on it. I wouldn't feel right, taking their time without paying them, and I couldn't afford that right now. "I don't know if this trend is going to last." Then there was the cost of supplies. "For all I know, those people this morning were the only ones interested."

As if the universe didn't appreciate being challenged, the Addams Family theme filled the shop when someone walked in. "Hello?" they called out. "I'm here about the furniture that was on Adam's Weird Menagerie?"

There wasn't much breathing or thinking room, as people continued to trickle in over the next few hours.

When Dylan got in, Adam and Brooke vanished downstairs together.

I wanted to follow, but I was negotiating with a woman about my age on the cost of an old trunk.

My being busy didn't stop my mind from wandering over what kind of things could happen down there when two people were left unattended. The stab behind my ribs wasn't the *j*-word. Nope.

I was just concerned about my friends.

9

adam

"I DON'T KNOW that you'd make a great Lara Croft."

Brooke looked at me, brows raised. "Excuse me?" She didn't sound upset. More confused.

I hadn't spent a lot of time with her without Deacon being here, so I didn't know her well. The thing I tried to hide from most people was that I was socially awkward. I never said the right thing at the right time. "Your polygon count is too high."

Her laugh wasn't one of those *how stupid are you* laughs. It sparkled in her eyes and lit up her face. "And here I thought you were going to tell me I didn't look enough like Angelina Jolie."

"I mean, you don't, but that's not bad." I should quit while I was ahead. I pointed to the wall that ran between Deacon and Aubrey's shop. "Breaker box is straight up."

"Should be easy enough to get to. How likely do

you think it is that these walls are up to code, as is? Because I can't bury electrical in this stone."

"Do you have to bury it?"

Now Brooke looked puzzled. "I guarantee leaving wires exposed won't pass inspection."

"No, but what about hiding them under something like hollowed out trim?" I followed the wall to one corner, doing a moderate check of moisture and trying to gauge temperature. It wasn't an exact science; I'd still need to do things properly. But this would give me an idea of what kind of work was needed down here, to make the place customer friendly. "I don't think we have to put new walls over the existing stone."

When Brooke didn't answer, I turned back to see her face drawn in thought.

"That's kind of brilliant, actually. Easy to get to. Easier to move once Deacon has more time to figure out what he wants as a finished product." She grinned. "I like it."

This would be easy. Depending on Brooke's timeline, we could have Deacon sending customers down here within a week. "I need something to sketch this out on. Possible points to set up walls."

Brooke rummaged in the oversized bag hanging from her shoulder and pulled out a notebook and pen.

"You have a Mary Poppins bag. Nice." I took the offering and started counting off steps toward the middle of the room.

"It's not quite as good as Mary Poppins's bag, but I have a Mom-purse, so close enough." She walked beside me. "Are you a Tomb Raider fan?"

"I'm a fan of anything even remotely archeological, especially when guns and ancient, vengeful spirits are involved. But my older brother..." The memories rushed back with unexpected potency. The downside to the therapy I'd started recently was that so much of the past floated near the surface, after I'd successfully ignored it for years. "Brandon loved the game. He taught me how to play."

Seven-year-old me, sitting next to my *grown-up* fifteen-year-old brother, who had the patience of a saint back then, just knew I was the coolest second grader ever, as he coaxed me through each level.

I dusted away the discordant blend of happiness and bitterness.

"You okay?" Brooke asked.

"I'm fine. Sometimes the past just catches up to me, you know?"

For a heartbeat, sadness tinged her expression. "I do." She shook her head. "So, walls. Where can we put them?"

We spent the next hour figuring out where changes needed to be made and where additional updates could be made, and sketching it all out.

The longer Brooke and I worked together, the more I found myself watching her, rather than my sketches. The way she tucked her hair behind one ear and caught the tip of her tongue between her teeth when she was thinking was simple but enthralling. Talking to her was easy; she understood my references, and I got hers.

Plus, she was fucking gorgeous.

So this was why Deacon was fixated on her.

Which was fine. He needed to close the deal with her, and I was just enjoying the scenery and the company.

When we had a good idea of what we needed to do, we headed upstairs to find Deacon.

He was selling the last piece we'd brought up this morning, a beautifully carved wooden dildo, to a man who looked like someone's great grandfather.

To each their own.

There were two more interruptions while Brooke and I walked Deacon through our proposal, but the customers left their information and walked out when we told them there wouldn't be more available until later.

We finally finished explaining what it would take to make the basement ready for customers.

"How much will it cost?" Deacon asked.

I couldn't charge him for this. "Cost is negligible."

He sighed. "*Negligible* doesn't sign checks or pay bills."

"I've got a lot of this stuff in storage." Not the wood, but the rest.

"And I have most of what I need at home," Brooke said.

I was glad we were on the same page. This was

about helping Deacon, even if it cost a little out of our own pockets.

Deacon frowned. "No. I want receipts when you're done. You're not footing the bill for my upgrades. Neither of you."

I stared back.

"Promise me," he said.

I'd been living here rent free since I lost my place, because Deacon refused to take my money. "Anything that costs more than I owe you in back rent, I'll give you receipts for. Labor is free, and you need this work done."

"The money conversation isn't over, but you're right. I need to get people down there." Deacon scrubbed his hand over his head. "Let's do—"

"Mister Onassis." A new arrival interrupted in a tone that sounded too much like Hugo Weaving's *Mister Anderson* for my taste. Travis Paddock was on the city council and had led the push for the regulations that had Deacon stressed about whether or not he'd get to keep his shop.

"I believe this is your store, featured in this film?" He shoved a tablet in Deacon's face, and my voice played, sounding tinny coming from the speakers. Cool. It was my video from last night.

Deacon raised an eyebrow. "You know it is."

"There are at least three violations of the new code in the way this was posted."

Bullshit. "The new code doesn't go into effect for a month. Besides, it's my video, and you can't control what other people post online about this street." I wouldn't let Deacon take the blame for this, especially when there was no blame to be had.

"Except that you live and work here. You're not a random visitor." Travis sneered. "And some of the items in this clip violate current zoning. You're not allowed to sell adult products and sex toys."

This man was Level Fifty intolerable, but until I figured out how to 3D print a phaser, I was pretty sure I couldn't disintegrate him without getting caught.

"They're not adult toys; they're antiques." Brooke was much more eloquent than I was, but the tightness in her reply was unmistakable.

Travis turned his gaze on her, as if seeing her for the first time since he arrived, and a sickly smile slithered onto his face. "Sister Doyle. You don't want to associate yourself with these people."

Sister Doyle? Okay, asshole.

"It's *Brooke*. *Ms. Mansell-Doyle* if you insist on being formal." She definitely sounded annoyed. "And these are exactly the types of men I want to associate myself with."

I wanted to stick my tongue out, and say, *Nyah, so there*. This was why I shouldn't interact with the general public.

Travis clucked and shook his head. "Poor, naive Brooke. You have no idea what he's selling here, do you?"

I definitely wanted to disintegrate this guy, and

Deacon's clenched fist said he was considering a more tangible approach.

In contrast, a sweet smile spread across Brooke's face. "I do know. I got a hands-on demonstration last night."

Wait. What?

10
brooke

I SHOULDN'T HAVE SAID that. Why did I say that?

I didn't care if Travis knew that I'd had any sort of intimacy with Deacon; I saved terms like *hate* and *loathe* for the severest of people, but I detested Travis Paddock. He'd pretended he cared about my grief, then pursued me without pause a year or so after my husband passed away.

But telling Travis anything was the equivalent of hanging large banners on every shopfront on Main Street.

Worse, the look on Adam's face was somewhere between shock and hurt.

No one was saying anything, but everyone was staring at me. What was I supposed to do now?

I gave a light laugh that sounded fake to my own ears. "Just kidding. But don't insult my intelligence like that again. I don't believe you have the power to walk in here and shut things down because you see perversion where most people see a chair."

Travis's nostrils flared. "This is not a game, and I'm not a cliché movie villain, trying to steal your livelihood. You can't sell those things under current zoning, and it will be on the docket at the next council meeting, Mr. Onassis."

"I look forward to arguing my case." Deacon's reply was smooth, and his expression blank. "You can find your way out?"

"Brooke." Travis nodded at me before he left.

"Freaking asshole," I muttered as the door swung shut behind him.

For the second time in as many minutes, I was met with twin expressions of shock. "Sorry."

"Never apologize," Deacon said. "And *bravo*, by the way. I can only think of a few things sexier than the way you put him in his place."

I ducked my head, not sure how to respond. Was he teasing me? Did it mean more? After last night...

Which I was supposed to remember didn't mean anything beyond the physical. No reason to read more into Deacon's words than I did before.

"Speaking of, but not really—" Adam's tone drew my attention. "Was there or was there not a hands-on lesson last night?" he asked. "Because that denial wasn't exactly convincing."

It really wasn't, was it? *Oh geez.* Wait. If Adam didn't know, Deacon wasn't talking about it. Out of respect, or because what we did didn't matter?

Nope. I wasn't going to fall into endless questions when I'd been given an answer. "It was just a lesson."

"The orgasms-and-no-clothes kind of lesson?" Adam asked.

I couldn't do this. Yesterday, I couldn't talk about sex without blushing, and that hadn't changed. There was no way I could casually toss out an answer in the same tone I might use when ordering food at a drive-through.

"There were both clothes and orgasms." Deacon could. But I knew that.

Adam stared at him. "Dude."

There was minimal inflection in the word. Was it praise? Disbelief? Something else?

"Dude." Deacon shrugged.

Adam shook his head. "Don't do that. Don't *Baseketball* me."

I assumed he meant the movie.

"You started it, and when was I going to tell you?" Deacon asked. "Today has been insane." He looked at me. "Not that I plan on running around telling the world. What happened is between you and me."

Which I understood, but also, I felt like I wasn't quite part of this conversation. "He's your best friend. I get it." I wasn't going to be the clingy person who didn't understand the meaning of *we're just friends*. Travis did that to me, once upon a time. And had the nerve to tell me he invested all that time in our friendship, so I owed him at least one date.

"And now that the room knows about last night, what are we doing in the basement?"

I winced at the phrasing of my question, because I wanted to follow it with, *More of what we did last night?*

"I can't make changes like this without a plan." Deacon really did have this under control. "Especially not if Travis has set his sights on the shop. Let's finalize your plans."

We dug through the details of what we needed to do, and the conversation shifted to dry details for a while.

"Do you think he's jealous?" Adam asked out of nowhere.

"Who?" Deacon sounded puzzled.

But I had a pretty good idea. "Travis."

"Of the basement." Adam worked up a model on his laptop of the proposed work while we talked.

Deacon shook his head. "Because he needs more kink in his life?"

"Probably." My answer slipped out before I could consider it. Like I was one to talk.

Adam tapped a series of keys, made a few mouse clicks, and sat back to show us the screen. "But also because he's a basement dweller, and that's a kick ass basement."

I laughed. "I don't have an argument. Zero."

"I dunno. I know some pretty nice basement dwellers. It feels like an affront to them to lump them in the same category." Deacon leaned in to flip through Adam's work. "This is perfect. Let's do it."

"We can start bringing in supplies first thing in the morning." I already had a list in my head of what I needed from my workshop. "My tools won't fit in my car, though."

"I have that problem all the time." Deacon's voice was light mixed with an exaggerated smoothness.

Adam exported his work to a pretty single file, and attached it to an email. "It's why he drives the *big* truck."

"Totally not because I'm over-compensating. Wink wink," Deacon teased.

"Pretty sure you weren't over-compensating last night." Was I allowed to say that? The playfulness should be easy, but now things were different.

Or were they?

Adam worked his jaw. "That's what she said?" His laugh was tight.

"Exactly. And she's not the kind of woman to tell a lie," Deacon said smoothly. "And I can swing by in the morning and pick up whatever you need brought back here."

How did he do that? I was definitely going to need another lesson, or three, to figure out the nuances of this casual sex thing.

"Sounds like a plan." I caught a glimpse of the clock on Adam's laptop, and disappointment swam in. "Speaking of, I should get home." I trusted my kids to be home alone without me, find food, and not wreck the house, but I liked to be around to hear about their day when I could, unless I'd warned them first. "First thing tomorrow?"

"*Yes.*" Adam sounded excited.

Deacon clenched his jaw. "My *first thing*, not his."

"Aww. The day will be half over by then." Adam's pout was exaggerated.

I laughed again, waved over my shoulder, and headed outside. The highs and lows—but mostly the highs—of the day hummed under my skin, mingling with memories of last night. Adam was a lot of fun to hang out with, and he was cute. And aside from my doubt, Deacon was as tempting as ever.

As I was sliding into my car, my phone rang and I fished it out of my purse. "Hello," I answered.

"Who are you and what have you done with Brooke?" It was Carly, and her tone was playful.

I'd been torn when I texted her this morning between a long explanation and simple request. I'd gone with simple, and apparently chosen wrong. Though, was there really a right answer? "I'm still me, I promise."

"More spanking books? You're not you."

I laughed at her exaggerated disbelief. "I'm trying new things." Would it be obvious I was trying them in real life as well? I wasn't ready to surrender that information again. "In my reading." Way to be subtle, me. Not.

"Reeaaally." Carly drew the word out with a

chuckle. "Do you want to add anything besides *spanking* to the list? Expand your horizons wider?"

I didn't even know where to start. There were so many things in Deacon's basement that I hadn't realized were real or had never even heard of. There was one thing I liked a lot last night, though. "Restraints? Like handcuffs?"

"Bold woman, I like it. What else?"

"I have no idea. What else is there?"

Carly blew out a loud puff that echoed in my ear. "Your options run the gamut. Wax. Public sex. Humiliation. Knife play. Edging."

I could picture what most of those phrases meant from a dictionary stand-point, and I felt like I was tip-toeing in the kiddie pool while Carly was trying to get me to high-dive into the deep end of the Olympic-sized pool. "Wax? Like… wax lips?"

"Like candles. The hot wax leaves a little bit of burn on the skin and can paint pretty colors."

"Burning sounds bad."

"It's not like a third-degree burn," Carly said. Her tone softened. "It's enough heat to sting but still be yummy."

There were so many things I wanted to learn. The books would help, but I wanted hands-on demonstrations about each and every one I read about. I wasn't quite ready to go all in, though. "I'm skipping the wax for now, but spanking and handcuffs…"

"You've got it, lady. I'll send you a list."

"Thank you." I was grinning as I hung up. This

has been a good day, and the next few seemed like they'd be even better.

I slid into my car, fit the key in the ignition, and turned.

Nothing happened.

11
deacon

Brooke walked back into the shop moments after she left, and I couldn't help my smile. She didn't look as happy, though. "My car won't start. I'm sorry for the trouble, but maybe I could get a ride home? If not, I can call one of the kids, it's no big deal, but since I'm here and you're here, and—"

"It's not any trouble, of course you can." I had to stop her before she rambled herself into justification-oblivion. Besides, a ride home meant alone time, and possibly seeing if the worktable in her shed was sturdy enough for—

"We could all go," Adam said. "Load up the tools tonight. It'll be faster with more hands."

Did he just... No. He didn't cock block me because she simply asked for a ride home. Besides, his suggestion made sense—a few of the things we needed to bring back here were going to take some lifting and maneuvering to get them into the truck without hurting anything or anyone.

Brooke grinned. "You could stay for dinner if you did that. It's Bryan's night to cook, and I'm pretty sure he made jambalaya."

"Not that you owe us anything, but that sounds pretty good." I was all in for someone else's cooking.

My '85 F-150 was older than I was, and the bench seat was more than big enough for all three of us. Brooke sat nestled between Adam and me, her arm pressed into mine and the heat tempting me, on the ride back to her house.

We parked next to the large shed that was her sculpting and welding workshop. "Come inside, eat first, then we can do the hard work," she said.

We followed her into the house.

"I'm home," she called.

Brooke owned a farmhouse that looked faithfully restored from the outside, from the wood siding all the way down to the color of the trim and paint. Inside was a different story. She'd kept the original hardwood, but there wasn't a flowered couch or doily anywhere to be found.

Her sculptures decorated the mantle, her brother's art hung on several of the walls, and most other free spaces were filled with pictures of her kids and their various awards. The furniture was eclectic and well-worn, though the place was pretty clean.

I liked it—it always felt to me like people lived

here who loved each other and living life, rather than feeling like a showroom piece.

"Is that Deacon's truck?" Paige's question came from upstairs. "Did you finally convince—" She came into view and froze on the top step. "Oh. Hello."

Adam waved. "Hello."

I smiled at the unfinished question. Paige had been trying to convince me for months to let her make some *modifications* to my truck. I needed it for work, and couldn't afford to have it out for several days just because. "No, she didn't. Especially considering her car is sitting dead in my parking lot."

"What? No." Paige joined us in the living room. "Not my fault. What's it doing?"

Brooke described the symptoms, and Paige's frown grew. "It was acting funny yesterday on the drive down to the shop, and then *bam* no start."

"Okay. I'll borrow the tow truck from Mr. Brown tomorrow morning and bring the car back to the school auto shop," Paige said.

"How long will I be without?" Brooke hung up her coat, then took ours and hung them on empty pegs by the door.

Paige was the one restoring Brooke's Bel Air. "Based on what you described, it's probably the timing chain, though it might be the transmission slipping. Either way, a couple of days at least."

"Or it's the distributor cap or wires," Adam said.

Paige's scowl reminded me of Brooke. "I replaced

both just a few months ago. She doesn't exactly drive it into the ground."

"True. But parts can be bad, and it takes two minutes to check." Adam didn't necessarily work on cars, but he'd been an office manager at a repair shop for a while, and he had a head full of random mechanical knowledge.

She sighed. "People rarely get that lucky. Unlucky? But fine, I'll check."

"*Hey*," Bryan shouted from the other room. "You're supposed to be setting the table, Paige."

"*Sorry*." She looked at me. "Think about it. Tell me what I have to do to get that truck into the school's garage."

I shook my head. "Nothing. Not any time in the foreseeable future. Not happening."

"Fine." Paige huffed and headed into the kitchen.

"Set two extra spots," Brooke called after her.

I always felt a twinge when I visited Brooke's, or anywhere that her kids were around. An echo of a life I used to want so badly. When I was in my early twenties, I'd been engaged to the woman I swore was the love of my life. When she told me she was pregnant, I was thrilled. I was going to have a family, we were going to do everything right, and it was going to be amazing.

And when I found out she was carrying twins, I'd been over the moon.

About seven months into the pregnancy, I found out she'd been cheating on me. With my supposed best friend, for ages, and she was leaving me for him. There was no way I was letting her take my kids away from me. We'd work out custody, I'd still raise them and love them and give them the best life.

Except blood tests showed they weren't mine.

Like that, my plans for the future had evaporated.

I could look back and see that it was for the best, that I was happy being the guy who didn't tie himself down to any one person. Still, seeing Brooke with her twins always whispered *what if...* in my ear.

"Come on, let's eat." Brooke tugged us into the kitchen.

The table and chairs were from my shop, and were one of the few sets that matched the house they sat in. We took our seats, and dug into the food.

"How were your days?" Brooke asked.

Both kids had generic answers along the lines of *fine.*

How strangely normal was this?

"Oh, Mom." Paige was suddenly excited. "Jamie and me—"

"Jamie and I," Bryan cut her off.

Paige rolled her eyes, finishing with a glare at her brother. "We can tell your story in a minute."

"That's not what I—"

"That's not what *me* meant." She stuck her tongue out. "I know what you meant, grammar nerd."

Bryan clenched his jaw. "You sound more intelligent when—"

"I'm intelligent regardless of my fucking language."

There wasn't enough malice in either twin's voice for me to feel like this was a real argument, and instead, it was entertaining to watch.

"What did you and Jamie do, Paige?" Brooke brought the conversation back to its starting point, like a true master. That was kind of sexy.

Paige was all grins again. "We found the perfect dresses for the Sweetheart's dance, and the perfect suit for Bryan, too. He's going with us."

"Aubrey has an honest-to-God zoot suit." Bryan's enthusiasm was back, too.

Paige's eyes turned wide, in what I assumed was her go-to *mom will cave for this* look. "Can we buy them, please? I'll do whatever chores you want."

"Must be an amazing dress." I figured it had to be, given the immediate shift in her mood, after taking good-natured grief from her brother. Though to be fair, most things Aubrey sold were pretty cool.

"So. Amazing. She's got these flapper dresses, and there are these boots—"

"Tell her boots don't go with dresses." Bryan interrupted again. "Don't let her get the boots, Mom."

Adam set his fork down. "Boots go with anything if you know how to rock the look. My brother's girlfriend is living proof."

Paige pointed emphatically at him. "See? If Reese Fucking Ellis does it, it's cool."

Brook winced, I suspected at the language, but she

didn't correct Paige. Though Brooke didn't swear much herself, she'd reached a point where she tried to let her kids be adults and make their own decisions, and that included about their language.

"How much?" Brooke asked.

Paige's wince looked a lot like Brooke's. "Three hundred for all of it." Her reply was meek.

"Both dresses, plus the boots and the suit?"

Paige nodded. "Plus jewelry. It's not real, but it looks really good with the dresses. I'll fix your car."

"You're fixing my car regardless."

"Bryan and I will do spring prep for the entire property next month."

Bryan's jaw dropped. "*Hey.*"

Paige fixed him with a look. "Do you want the suit?"

"We'll do it," Bryan agreed.

Brooke nodded. "It's a deal. You can use the card, as long as it's just for dance outfits."

"Yay." Paige clapped.

Bryan's pleased smile was more reserved, but I suspected he was just as happy.

This was both disturbingly and soothingly sweet. I liked that Brooke managed to be a parent, but still let her kids make a lot of their own decisions. I respected and admired that, even though this whole vibe wasn't for me.

Conversation faded while we ate. Adam and I both knew the basics of cooking, enough that we didn't have to get take out every day and didn't burn the house down when we used the stove, but this was a different level of home cooking than I was used to. It was really good.

"Before I forget," Brooke said as we were finishing eating. "I may be out late tomorrow, helping Deacon with some wiring in his shop. If I'm not home when you're done with school, fend for yourselves."

"Oh, in the basement?" Bryan lit up. "Can we come by and see the new furniture?"

How much did they know about what we'd found?

Brooke shook her head. "Not until the place is up to code. Or possibly never while I'm alive."

"We already know what's down there. We saw it on Adam's channel." Bryan sounded like he believed his logic was inarguable.

I didn't have to look at Adam to know he was fighting a smirk at the reach of his newly found fame.

Brooke shot both of us a look that was half-glare, half-*help*, and I shrugged. "Like you told Travis— they're antiques. That's what I sell."

Paige snorted.

"We need to get some stuff from my shed into Deacon's truck." Brooke pushed back from the table. "Dinner was great, thank you, Bryan."

Both kids looked disappointed at the end of the conversation, but they started clearing the table without prompting.

Adam, Brooke, and I headed outside.

"I'm not prepared for things like my kids

exploring sex toys," Brooke muttered, then looked at me with wide eyes, as if she'd just realized she said that aloud. She cleared her throat and unlocked the shed. "Those are the tools we need." She pointed to a few larger items, and a large toolbox.

"The twins obviously have the internet." I should let this go, but I had thoughts on her comment. "As long as you've had *the talk* with them, they'd probably rather just know they can come to you with problems and not have you judge them. If you've explained *this is how babies are made* and *consent good, internet porn unrealistic*, I suspect they don't want to hear you explain sex toys any more than you want to explain them."

Brooke's laugh was tinged with exasperation. "You're probably right. Something to be grateful for, I guess?" She grabbed a smaller, metal box, and followed us outside to load things into the bed of the truck.

"Would it make you feel better if I gave them a PG tour of the basement when things are in a place where the public is allowed down there?" I fitted everything in place without much thought, and we went back for the rest.

"It would make me feel better if they weren't curious at all, but I suppose they're too old for me to hope that." She stopped in the middle of the room and puffed out a sigh, blowing a few loose strands of hair out of her face. "Would you be okay with that?"

"Of course."

"You're the best, thank you."

It was basic praise, but it warmed me from the inside out.

We finished loading the truck and Adam and I headed out. The night played on repeat in my mind, despite me wanting to move on. Brooke's family wasn't mine, and I could respect her and her situation without wanting to be a part of it.

I'd moved past wanting that life, and I was happy with what I had.

12
adam

"You and Brooke. It's really nothing?" Why did I interrupt a perfectly comfortable, conversationless trip back to Deacon's with a question like that?

"Yes." Deacon didn't hesitate. "I fully expect she's spending her nights sifting through countless suitors, and I hope she's finding at least one or two she can swipe right on. She deserves a happily ever after. She deserves a lot more than I'm offering."

That was a lengthy answer, but it didn't matter because it didn't impact me either way. "Okay."

A loose thought, related but just out of my grasp, floated at the edges of my mind. I tried to reach it, but it kept slipping away just as I got close.

My therapist could probably drag the reality out of me, but some days being analyzed and picked apart was draining. My mother had walked out on my father because they'd lied to themselves and each other about wanting the same things from their futures, and she finally admitted it when Baby Adam arrived.

This wasn't the same at all. It was the opposite of a relationship. Besides Deacon and Brooke were adults who could make their own decisions, but I didn't want to see either of them hurt.

When we got to the antique shop, Deacon and I spent the next few hours unloading the truck and making sure the basement was set for work tomorrow morning. We wrapped up and he stopped to clear out the store's voicemail. There were several more people asking about the things from the video.

He asked me to change the message to let people know nothing was currently available, but there would be more soon, and he returned calls to tell them the same thing.

I finished before he did, and was waiting to see if he needed anything else when the shop phone rang. "Deacon's Derelicts and D'Art," I answered.

"Hi. I'm looking for the guy who posted the video about your shop last night?"

I doubted he really wanted to talk to me, but I was happy to field any questions I could about the new pieces. "That's me."

"Hey. It's Adam, right? This is Sebastian from down the street."

"The new age tea shop, right? Hey. If you have questions about the furniture, Deacon can answer them better than me, but he'd probably give you a first look."

Deacon glanced at me at the mention of his name, but went back to his call.

"I'm actually looking for you," Sebastian said. "I have a few high-end pieces here that are really more to draw attention than to sell, though I wouldn't mind if someone paid for them. Would you be up for doing a similar video for me?"

That sounded cool. "Sure. I can't guarantee you'll get the same kinds of hits as the secret sex dungeon, but I'd be happy to."

"I've got crystals that are supposed to cure impotency, and others that are dildos, how's that for a draw?"

It was pretty good. We set up a time for me to head over on Sunday, and hung up.

Too cool. I should see if Aubrey was interested in the same. Maybe a few more of the shops on the block. Make an entire series that extended beyond Deacon's, though the antique shop would have to stay the focus overall.

This was going to be fun.

BROOKE SHOWED up in the morning an hour before we opened, coffee in one hand and box of pastries in the other. "I thought we might need brain food today."

"You're a genius. And an angel. A beautiful genius angel." I took the box from her, grabbed a cheese

Danish, and set the rest on the counter. "I didn't expect you so early. Deacon just got up."

"The kids dropped me off on the way to school, but I couldn't sit at the coffee shop any longer. I need to be doing something."

"You're off to a great start." I grabbed another pastry and nodded toward the back room. "Do you want to head down there and get started?"

Her phone rang, and she glanced at the screen. "It's Paige. Hang on." She answered. "Hey. Shouldn't you be in second period?... That's fantastic, great job... Yeah, hang on." She held the phone out. "She wants to talk to you."

And here I was double fisting pastries like a five year old. I held up my full hands with a wince.

Brooke laughed and pressed the phone to my ear.

"Hello," I said.

"You were right about the wires." Paige sounded excited. "It worked, and the car runs... I have to go back to class now, which sucks, but everything's fixed."

"That's awesome. Way to go."

"Um..." Paige trailed off. "Could you maybe... I'm having a problem I can't figure out with my bike. Could you come by the house sometime and help?"

That sounded like fun. "I haven't done any work on motorcycles, but sure. Another set of eyes can't hurt."

"Thank you. Bye." Her smile was audible.

Brooke wrapped up the conversation with Paige,

and wrapped up with an easy *Love you*. It was both disconcerting and comforting to see how close their family was. I was on friendly terms with my brother, but our relationship was in a different universe from what Brooke and her kids had.

The two of us headed into the basement. For the next several hours, most of our conversation was limited to the tasks at hand, and had Brooke and I at opposite ends of the room. Deacon came down a few times, but there was enough business coming in today that he needed to stay upstairs and work with customers.

Watching her do her thing while she was in view was fascinating. There was no hesitation, and her fingers moved with an almost seductive skill and deftness.

As we drifted back together, I found myself watching her as much as working. The way she tucked loose strands of hair behind her ear, even though she wore a ponytail. How she caught her tongue between her teeth when she was focused. And especially the way her tone shifted toward brighter and stronger when she talked about something she was fascinated with—either the wiring or the last TV show she binged.

"You and Deacon…" The start of the question slipped out before I realized what I was about to ask. Not that I had any idea why I needed confirmation. I really should let this drop.

But her curious gaze stalled me. "What about us?"

I didn't know her nearly well enough to ask her, but here I was regardless. Wanting to know if she saw him as anything besides a fuck buddy. "The agreement the two of you have…"

"We're friends. That's all we are." Her answer came as quickly as his last night. "He's giving me lessons. Nothing more."

"Cool. Just curious." But it was more than that, wasn't it? What was I doing? Besides letting my mind drift more the longer I watched her. Wondering what it would be like to walk in one of those lessons. What it would be like to either help teach, or get to experience the results.

"Why?" Brooke's question caught me off guard.

It shouldn't have. It was a reasonable question. "Just looking out for friends."

"Okay." She turned back to her work.

"When did you lose your husband?" What was wrong with me today? There was awkward, and then there was just insensitive. "You've really been single the entire time since?" No, really. What was I doing?

The way Brooke was staring at me, I assumed she was thinking the same.

I shook my head. "I'm sorry. If I ever ask something inappropriate, just tell me to stop. I'm not made for casual conversation."

"It's okay." Her tone was light. "You surprised me, but I'd rather you said what was on your mind than what you thought I wanted to hear."

"I'm not very good at that second one. Mostly

because I'm so bad at figuring out what people want to hear." Human beings were odd and confusing creatures.

She pointed to the junction box she was working on. "I need a second set of hands. Can I borrow yours?"

Just tell me where to touch you. I wouldn't say that, because channeling Deacon wouldn't help me. "Sure."

"Hold these here." She pointed to two wires. "Don't let the tips touch."

My snort slipped out.

She raised her brows. "Penis joke?"

"It sounds both dirtier and not when you say *penis joke* instead of *dick joke*."

Brooke laughed. "I'll keep that in mind." She worked to attach the wires I was holding to the entire structure. "It's been a while. Since I lost my husband, that is. The twins barely remember him, and after he passed away I was focused on raising them." The catch in her voice was faint, but I recognized it because I sounded the same when my Dad came up.

"I have a hard time believing no one in this town was hitting on you."

"They were. Maybe someday, when I'm already pissed off and in a mood to make it worse, I'll tell you the story about Travis."

"I can't wait?"

This time her laugh was brighter. More real. "Over here next." She moved us to a new pair of wires.

"Seriously, the guy's a tool." Want whispered through me every time she brushed her hands over mine. How much longer could I ignore that? "A teensy tiny tool. Like the kind you get in one of those *home repair* gift sets, and the entire thing is so cheap that nothing in the box works except maybe the screwdriver, and it only works as a hammer."

Brooke's laughter grew—that was a pretty sound. "Is he the screwdriver, then?"

"Pretty sure he's the wire cutters. More likely to cut off the tip of your finger than do what he's actually supposed to."

"Another penis joke?"

I shook my head. "No, but now I wish it had been. I'm glad you didn't give him the time of day."

"Oh?"

"You deserve better than any schmuck in this town."

Pink tinged her cheeks. "You need to be at the same angle as me for this one." She pointed to a new spot. "Probably behind me."

I'd rarely wanted to hear someone say that more than I did right now, regardless of context. I moved to stand behind Brooke, and offered my arms. She guided me into place, and it took what little common sense I had to not push into her back.

"You and Deacon are in this town," she said softly as she worked.

I wouldn't lean in and smell her hair. That would

be creepy, but also prove my point. "But we're not really part of it. Also, we're still schmucks."

"You're really not. I need you closer."

And if I got too much closer, she'd feel my cock getting harder with each breath. I tried to find a compromise in following her instructions and not falling into how it felt to have my arms wrapped around her. "We could argue over how awesome I am, or you could tell me your favorite superhero movie."

I had enough self-awareness to know why I'd asked that. I wanted to shift away from a subject I never should have touched, and at the same time, find a reason to not be enthralled by Brooke.

"That depends." She worked quickly, as if she'd done this a thousand times before.

"On what?"

"Are we talking character development, action, or humor?"

Fuck, she was sexy. "You didn't include *plot* in that list."

She glanced over her shoulder, her smirk of disbelief close enough I could lean in and steal a kiss. "Nope." She turned back to her work. "And I'd leave it off again and again. All done."

Fantastic. Except that meant, "I suppose I have to let you go now." I shouldn't have said that aloud.

"Do you have to?" She turned, not dislodging my arms. She was so close. So tempting.

"Maybe not. This is pretty nice, isn't it?"

The way she studied me with those dark brown eyes that seemed to peer right into my soul, I swore she knew exactly what I was thinking.

"It really is." Her reply was breathy. She was so close. So stunning.

I slid a hand to her cheek and brushed my lips over hers. I shouldn't be doing this with her. Not with the sparks between her and Deacon. But if they were going to insist their relationship was friendship, and was she leaning into me rather than away?

I deepened the kiss, licking dust from her lips and memorizing how soft they were. She smelled like flowers and ozone, which was now officially my favorite scent. The soft gasp that escaped her chest drove straight to my groin.

"*Dude.*" Deacon's voice cut through the kiss.

Fuck. What was I doing?

13
brooke

"THIS ISN'T... It's not... It was a moment of weakness." Adam's denial sliced through me.

Especially since he still had me pinned to the wall, and that incredible kiss still buzzed through my entire body. I shoved him back enough to step away. "Sorry to be such a temptation." There was no apology in my tone, because screw that.

"No, I didn't mean... *Fuck*." Adam scrubbed his face and put a couple more feet between us.

"Paige dropped your car off. She said to be careful if you're out late, because it's supposed to snow." Deacon's tone was cool.

That was fine. Our relationship was only supposed to heat up during *class*. "Great. I can't do much more here until we can turn off the building power, so I'm going to head out." Lick my emotional wounds. Wonder why I let my defenses down for even a second with Adam.

Because things hadn't been that easy and carefree with anyone for a long time. Sure, there was heat with Deacon, but I still questioned so much. With Adam...

Apparently I hadn't questioned nearly enough.

Deacon handed me my keys without a word, and I headed toward the stairs.

"Don't." Adam's tone stopped me, even though the deceptive blend of request and sadness should've set me on high alert. "Neither of you can leave until the three of us talk through this."

Absolutely ridiculous. "Talk through what?"

"The fact that the tension in this room just cranked up by about a billion atmospheres."

Even being pissed off at Adam, I wanted to smile at his answer and how uniquely him it was.

"There's no tension." Deacon's ability to stay removed had been sexy less than forty-eight hours ago, and now it tore at me. "I was surprised, but I'm over it. Obviously Brooke was going to see other people, that was the point."

Obviously.

"I just didn't think it would be happening right under my feet. Or that it would start with kissing."

"It did with you." I turned to face them.

Deacon's smile was thin.

I had no idea what was happening. My insides were a mess, from my brain to my heart to my stomach. "I didn't think this was how our second lesson would go." I needed to rebuild some emotional walls. I thought they were solid, given they'd been in place for more than a decade, but all it took were a couple of kisses from a couple of gorgeous, fun, younger men, and I felt as exposed as if I'd been stripped bare.

That didn't bode well for my dating future.

"Both of you stop." Adam's voice was harder this time. "Don't say anything else yet, as much as I'd love some company in the *I really regret talking* category."

I stared at him, waiting.

Adam worked his jaw. He laughed nervously. "I didn't expect you to both listen. Brooke, it wasn't a lapse in judgment. I wanted to kiss you, and I'm not sorry I did."

Did Deacon just growl? A glance at him showed a casual expression and stance. I must have imagined the sound.

"How long do you need the power off?" Deacon asked.

And we were changing the subject. Fine. "Everything's in place. I really only need ten or fifteen minutes to hook it up to the main box if everything goes smoothly. More realistically, half an hour. If things go badly, an hour or more."

"I locked up before we came down here, but I'd like to make sure we don't impact Aubrey or anyone else on the block. We have a couple of hours to wait until the rest of the shops are closed." This wasn't Deacon. This was a pod person who had taken his place and didn't know how to make inappropriate jokes or tease me until I turned red or make my insides flutter from the attention.

And this definitely wasn't the Deacon I called a friend. I didn't understand how any of this *casual physical relationship* stuff worked at all. "Great. I'll be back then." I walked out before anyone could stop me. Not that anyone called my name.

As the jumble in my mind rearranged itself into words I could grasp, I stopped halfway up the stairs, turned around, and headed back. "This isn't right," I said as I approached them. "This isn't what I signed on for, and it's so far from what I wanted from *lessons* the other night that..." I'd what? "If I have to tell you both *no more touching* to get things back to normal, I will."

Adam raised his brows.

Deacon sighed. "I wasn't expecting what I saw. It's fine."

That kiss was better than *fine*. It was really good, and I wouldn't mind more of the same from Adam, more in general from him. My brain stumbled on the logic trap. Did that mean giving up lessons with Deacon? Was I about to come between friends? I'd never had to think about things like that before and I didn't know what to do next. "What now?"

So much for coming back to demand we make things better. I wasn't prepared to make good on my threat, but I didn't have a solution. Maybe if I'd waited for later lessons, I'd know how to handle *I want sex from two different men. Who also happen to be best friends.*

"Let's make this simple," Deacon said. "You have

to answer honestly, like Truth or Dare, but both at the same time."

"That would be Truth *and* Dare," Adam corrected him.

At least the snippet of banter felt familiar. "I think that's fair."

"Does anyone want to take anything back?" Deacon looked at each of us. "Kisses? Lessons? Anything along those lines?"

"No," I said at the same time Adam did.

Deacon nodded. "Me neither. I can only think of one solution."

I watched him, more than curious to hear his answer.

"All three of us sleep together."

Was that a thing? Rather, I knew some people did it—my brother was in love with two other people—but not me.

"Sometimes I forget what an asshole you are." Adam didn't sound as bothered as his words implied.

Deacon shrugged. "I didn't hear you offering a better idea, which is usually your thing."

It was an absolutely insane suggestion, but that didn't mean I hated it. The longer I thought about it, the more I liked the idea of more kisses from both of them. More touches. More… more. And all of it at the same time? The images lit my skin on fire. "I'm in."

Twin looks of shock greeted me, but Deacon recovered first. "See? Brooke's in."

"This is idiotic." Adam's chuckle was strained. "But Brooke's pretty smart, so if she's in, I'm in."

On numerous occasions, I'd been told things like *you're so pretty* as it related to my love life, but *pretty smart* was one of the sexiest things anyone had ever tossed out as a casual comment about me.

"And honestly, thank God." Adam closed the distance between us in a few short strides, and cupped my cheeks in his palms. "Because"— He crashed his mouth down over mine, swallowing my whimper of surprise and sending need coursing through me.

Using his full body, he guided me back until I collided with Deacon, who dug his fingers into my hips and pressed into me.

This was different in the most incredible way.

"Is there anything you want to try?" Deacon's question rumbled through my back.

I, uh... The naughtiest thing I'd ever done was give my husband a blow job and swallow. That seemed so tame compared to all of this.

"Another lesson for you." As Deacon spoke, he nudged up my shirt with his thumbs, and teased along the bare skin just above my waistband. "We'll help you figure out what you like, if you can learn to ask for what you want to try. Any man who doesn't want to hear what you want isn't worth your time."

Adam trailed a finger slowly down my chest. "There's something indescribably sexy about hearing someone say something like *spank me, please.*"

"That. That's what I want." I didn't even need to think about it. Not anymore than I had been for the last couple of days.

Deacon brushed the edge of my ear with his lips. "I think he wants to hear you say it."

This wasn't a big deal. They were words. They only held power if I gave it to them. But I was willing to give them a lot of power. "Spank me, please?" The taste was spicy and the potential for what they could summon coiled in my belly and flooded me with anticipation.

So did Adam's wicked, playful smirk.

"Just like that." Deacon's voice was thick.

Adam tangled his fingers with mine. "We should take this upstairs."

"We did it downstairs the other day." I wasn't picky about the location, but a teensy part of me was terrified that if we moved, this entire fantasy would fall apart, and I'd wake up to a much less sexy reality.

Adam tugged me gently toward the stairs. "You'll want to get comfortable for this."

"For you to slap my butt."

"Yes." He paused and leaned closer. "Because I promise it's going to sting."

Oh, geez. I was already more turned on than I thought possible, and we hadn't really started.

As we headed past the main floor and up to the second where Deacon's apartment was, I swore it was obvious what we were about to do.

It wasn't. I hung out here a bit and had a good

reason for being here today. There was nothing unusual, and it wasn't as if anyone was paying attention to us anyway.

That didn't stop me from feeling like I had a huge *I'm about to sleep with two men* neon sign flashing above my head. How was I going to do something I had a hard time even saying in my own head? I had no clue, but as much as my mind stumbled over the words, my body was humming with the desire to find out.

I was barely aware of what Deacon and Adam were saying when we got upstairs, because my pulse was hammering so hard in my ears. There was something about using Deacon's room because his bed was bigger, and he had that heavy headboard…

And now I was thinking about why that mattered, and I was straddling a wobbly, terrifying line between anticipation and anxiety.

"Hey." Deacon's heat against my back and his arms around my waist yanked me out of my thoughts and helped ground me. "You still here?"

Adam was in front of me, a gentle finger under my chin holding my gaze level with his. "You can stop any time. Now. Later. If it's too much. If it's not enough."

What I meant to be a casual laugh came out more as a nervous titter. "I can't imagine it not being enough."

"Something to feel fortunate about." Adam's voice was playful. He pressed his lips to my forehead.

Some of the knots inside me loosened. This was terrifying, but the men were acting so much more like themselves than what I'd seen in the basement when Deacon walked in on us. These were my friends. People I trusted. I didn't have the same agreement with Adam that I did with Deacon, but that just meant I was allowed to feel something for him.

I wasn't going to further muddy my thoughts with that kind of logic. Not now. But I didn't mind the possibility.

"Are you good?" Deacon's question was all concern.

I appreciated that he was checking in, like he did last time. "Yes."

And then they were stripping me out of my clothes a piece at a time, with so many tender kisses dotted in between. Part of me wanted to curl up and hide, not because of them, but because I was on display, naked in all my not-so-glory.

But the way Adam studied me, an easy smile tugging up his lips and appreciation in his eyes, lit my skin on fire. The way Deacon ran his hands over my body, over everything I thought was too wrinkly or pudgy or had stretch marks, and he never paused or pulled away, helped bolster my confidence.

Adam grasped my hand and led me to the bed. "Kneel on all fours."

If I didn't stop hesitating, tonight would never happen, but telling myself that didn't unstick my feet from the floor.

"The position always feels awkward when you start," Deacon said.

I looked at him. "Is that supposed to be reassuring?"

"Yes. You're not the only one who feels that way. But once you realize what's about to happen, the awkwardness is easy to ignore."

"Can we get to that part?"

Adam's chuckle was like strong, delicious fingers digging into me, and I couldn't help but comply.

Yup, it was definitely weird, being on all fours, naked with all my saggy bits sagging even more, in front of other people.

Adam leaned his head in next to mine, until we were cheek to cheek. "I'm going to keep this simple. If you want me to stop, at any point, you tell me so. Just like that."

I wasn't so sheltered that I didn't know what a safe word was, but I was grateful that tonight I didn't have to remember to use one, on top of everything else. I couldn't handle that.

Adam's hand cracked across my fleshy skin. The slap was loud and the sting made me whimper.

"Do you want me to keep going?" Adam asked.

It hurt, but I liked it. "Yes."

The next slap was on the other cheek, and it hurt just as much. The next couple were worse. But Then the sting lessened. A strange numbness set in. Adam paused every few strikes to glide his palm gently along the curve of my behind, which intensified my need. Increased the throbbing from my core. Made me wetter.

And then instead of withdrawing his hand for another slap, Adam slid between my legs. I gasped at the penetration when he slid inside me, and I was too wound up in all the sensations to do anything but drift toward his touch.

Deacon knelt next to me—I'd almost forgotten he was here—and cupped my breasts. He kneaded gently, then switched to rolling my nipples between his fingers.

I rocked between them, wrapped in bliss and floating in a kind of pleasure I'd never felt before.

Adam moved his other hand to my clit, and a new shock spilled over me. He teased and coaxed and nudged me into a climax that stole my thoughts and my breath and left my throat raw as Adam and Deacon eased their touches away.

Had I been screaming? I didn't know. I didn't care. *Wow.*

But there was something else I needed. As Deacon reached for me I said, "Wait."

14

adam

I SWORE my heart stopped when Brooke said *wait*. This woman... I wanted to do so many things to her. With her.

I knew I had a light sadistic streak, and I'd learned long ago how to find outlets for it—learned that destruction was best when it was followed by healing. And Brooke whimpering but begging for more... I wanted to hear that, to feel that, again and again.

How Deacon was relegating himself to *lessons* was beyond my comprehension.

But now she wanted us to wait.

"This is wonderful, but it'd be better if everyone was having orgasms," Brooke said.

And now she was sexier.

"What do you want next, in that case?" Deacon knelt next to her and looked her in the eye. "I know it feels awkward at first, but I promise you the dirty talk is hot, and it doesn't have to be flowery. *I want you to fuck me* works great."

Brooke shook her head. "I can't say those words normally. How am I supposed to string them together to say that?"

I pulled her into me, my hand on her stomach and her back molding to my front. I pressed my still-slick fingers to her lips.

She didn't hesitate to draw me in and suck herself from my fingers.

So. Good.

I trailed my lips up her neck. "Now you've got a dirty mouth. Might as well make the best of it."

Her laugh was light and carefree, and it was almost a guarantee that delicious sound was going to make me hard every time I heard it after tonight.

"I want to taste you, Deacon. I want you in my mouth." Brooke managed shy and direct in the same breath.

Deacon groaned a *fuck yes,* and I didn't blame him. He shifted his weight, not leaving the bed.

Brook clucked. "Clothes off. If I'm going to be naked, I get to see both of you, too." She kept getting hotter.

"Smart woman." I nipped her earlobe with a smirk.

Her soft sigh lit me up.

"So, can I...?" Brooke's hesitation was back.

"You won't know unless you ask," Deacon said.

"Can I have Adam inside me while I'm sucking on you?"

Fuck the Hell yes. "Don't go anywhere." I was reluctant to step away, but there were steps to be followed.

Brooke glanced over her shoulder at me. "Where am I going to go? Detroit?"

South Park reference. *Hot.* I slapped her lightly on the ass—really it was more of a tap—and her gasp was worth it.

Deacon and I undressed, and I rolled on a condom.

He settled on the bed near Brooke. She crawled toward him. I was captivated as she drew her tongue tentatively along the tip of his cock, and I groaned along with him when she took him in her mouth.

I knelt behind Brooke, and took the penetration so slowly it ached. But fuck it felt incredible, feeling her pussy around my shaft, slick and tight, encasing me until I was buried deep. Plus, she was making the most incredible sounds, and the way she was making Deacon's face contort with ecstasy was pretty good too.

The series of events were captivating. I needed to go slowly; it was so tempting to thrust and bust and blow my wad. Instead, I took my time withdrawing from Brooke before plunging back in again, teasing my fingers over her skin, and then moving back to her clit.

I stroked until her sighs became moans and then

stuttered cries. She pulled back from Deacon, and she was so deliciously loud when she came. She clenched around my cock as she ground back into me and let out a string of not-quite *oh, God*s.

It took the last of my restraint to keep from not bursting right then.

As her orgasm ebbed, she ducked her head and returned to sucking Deacon off with full enthusiasm. Though I couldn't see her face, I had a perfect image of the sweetness Deacon saw when she looked at him and pleaded, "In my mouth?"

Jesus. This woman.

Deacon wrapped one fist around his cock and knotted the other in her hair and guided her head back down.

Brooke ground against me as she worked Deacon to the point his head tilted back and his grunts grew punctuated. The familiar sound of his climax, combined with Brooke's warm, wet pussy sheathing me, was almost too much. I gripped her hips tightly, needing something to focus on besides release.

Brooke pulled away from Deacon, and he shuddered as he slid from her mouth. Her giggle was one of self-satisfaction.

I was done holding back. I slammed inside her fast and hard, my body already clenching in anticipation. Desire spilling through my veins, coiling in my gut, and tightening in my balls. I needed to feel Brooke clench around me one more time, so I sought out her clit again. It didn't take much to draw another orgasm from her, and *fuck* the sensation was delicious.

The world slowed to a vibrant, lazy technicolor when I came, dancing behind my clenched eyelids as orgasm spilled from me.

I kept thrusting until I couldn't anymore, then leaned forward to kiss along Brooke's back.

The three of us collapsed in a pile and lay there for a moment catching our breath. I had the presence of mind to extract myself long enough to clean up and help Brooke do the same, but then I was content to fall back under the blankets with both of them.

We should get up again soon. Get dressed. Head into the basement and finish the wiring.

But that meant letting go of Brooke and leaving behind the warmth of Deacon. That meant covering up the stunning red handprints on her ass. Fuck, I hope she thought of me every time she sat down over the next day or two.

"We should get back to work." The reluctance in her voice matched mine.

A loud boom sounded outside, and a second later the lights blinked out. My heart hammered against my ribs at the abrupt sound. "What the fuck?"

"It's that stupid transformer down the street." The mattress shifted as Deacon climbed from the bed.

The only light in the room was a pale glow coming in around the curtains, making it impossible to see even my own hand in front of my face. As Deacon drew closer to the window, the soft gleam cast his naked form in a hauntingly beautiful silhouette. If I had my camera, I'd want to capture the sight.

He opened the curtains and bathed the whole room in the eerie gray of snow and clouds reflecting off each other. "Power's out on the whole street."

I sighed loudly and flopped my weight back against the pillows, pulling Brooke with me. Her surprised giggle was musical.

"Can't do much without power—except conserve body heat—we should probably stay in bed." I was brilliant if I did say so myself.

Brooke clucked. "Tempting. *Really* tempting."

"You're not going anywhere else for a while anyway." Deacon was still staring out the window. "Somehow we fucked our way into a blizzard."

"I think I saw that movie. We need to be careful, because the horny zombies are coming for us," I said.

Deacon turned to face us, laughing. "Coming for us, or *coming* for us?"

"They're zombies, so eww." Brooke scrunched up her face. "I mean, unless that's your thing, I guess?"

"I definitely prefer my groans to come from the living." I nipped her shoulder with my teeth, and she rewarded me with the most delicious sound.

She extracted herself from my arms and moved to the edge of the bed. "I should call the kids. Make sure they're all right."

"Tell them you probably won't be home tonight," Deacon said.

Brooke plucked her clothes from where they'd

landed, wrinkled her nose when she grabbed her panties, and just tugged on her shirt and jeans. "Because of the snow."

"That too." I grinned. The moment might have been interrupted, but now there was a chance for more fun later. Snow days were the best.

Deacon and I dressed, and he called the power company while Brooke called home. I went in search of candles.

They found me before I found what I was looking for. If Deacon didn't have candles, I did. We'd repurpose them for the night.

"Power company says ETA is at least tomorrow morning," Deacon said.

"I guess we'll have to cuddle to keep warm." I didn't mind the idea of that.

Deacon gestured to the wood burning stove in the corner of the kitchen. "And maybe haul some wood up, for that. Not that I have much."

"We should make sure everyone else on the block is set for a night without power," Brooke said.

Not every shop owner on the street lived above their place like Deacon, but several of them did. We bundled up and headed outside. A few of the neighbors were already out here—Aubrey, Sebastian, and others I'd only met a couple of times.

Fortunately, Travis the Tool was probably home safe and sound in his house on the hill, because his trollish face might ruin the gorgeous still that was out here tonight.

After a brief exchange, everyone agreed they were set for tonight, and they all promised no one would be freezing to death.

Sebastian had an actual fireplace, and invited anyone over who needed it.

As we turned to head back in, Brooke slipped and let out a horrible and heart-wrenching whimper of pain.

15
deacon

THE SOUND BROOKE made sliced through me worse than the cold. She was on the ground in more than a foot of snow, cringing and struggling to find her footing.

I offered her a hand and tugged her to her feet. She let out a yelp when she put her weight on the right one, and I wrapped an arm around her waist before she could stumble again, and Adam was at her other side without hesitation.

"I'm sorry." She sounded forlorn.

I held her upright. "Don't be."

"It hurts. Enough that I'm thinking about swearing."

I wanted to kiss the hurt away. Nothing deep-throat, tonsil-tickling, but something sweeter, like a peck on the cheek or the forehead kiss Adam gave her earlier. But that hardly felt like a *just friends* kind of gesture.

"Don't try to walk on it." Sebastian joined us. He'd been an EMT before he inherited his shop from his grandmother. "Get her inside."

I scooped Brooke into my arms, and her surprised gasp sounded too much like the sounds she'd made when she was being spanked. She relaxed in a breath, molding herself to my chest. This was both way better and far worse than the gasp on its own.

I shook my reactions aside, carried her into the shop, and set her gently on a stool behind the counter.

Adam used his phone to light the path after we left the brightness of the snow behind.

"Didn't even get winded. I'm impressed." Sebastian clapped me on the shoulder.

Adam stood at Brooke's side. "He is. He's just too manly to let it show."

I raised my brows, not trusting myself to speak without gasping for air.

Adam and I offered the best light we could with our phones, while Sebastian checked Brooke's ankle, prodding and twisting gently and asking her if it hurt after each movement. At his request, I stepped away long enough to grab an ace bandage, and pack some snow into a storage bag.

I wanted to run into the basement and grab the battery powered lights as well, but I wasn't sure where we'd left them and stumbling around in limited light, in the cold, was a bad idea.

When I returned, Sebastian wrapped her foot up with the bandage. "Ninety-nine percent sure it's a mild sprain. Nothing looks like it's broken or cracked, but keep your weight off it for the next couple of days, elevate it when you can, ice it as often as you need, and make sure you get to a doctor for a second opinion."

"Thank you." Brooke gave him a warm smile.

"No problem. You know where to find me if you need me." Sebastian gave a wave, and headed out.

As soon as he was gone, Brooke hopped from the stool, landing on her good foot.

"Whoa," I said at the same time as Adam. "What did you not understand about staying off your feet?" I asked.

The look Brooke gave me lacked any apology. "He told me to keep my weight off it. I am. What are you going to do, carry me everywhere?"

"If I have to." I wasn't going to let her make the injury worse.

Would I go to this kind of effort if Aubrey was the one who was hurt? Or Adam?

Of course I'd be this protective of Adam. Where did the thought come from? "What are you off to do, anyway? We can't go anywhere."

"I'm going to use the toilet. And our relationship —whatever it is—is not in a place where you're carrying me into the bathroom and waiting while I finish."

That was fair. "Wait thirty seconds." I strode away at a quick pace, and returned with a cane I'd fetched from a bin of them. "But then we're going upstairs, and you're staying there the rest of the night."

Brook studied me, contemplation written on her face. "All right."

When we made it upstairs, we decided putting her in Adam's room made the most sense—it was closest to the bathroom and kitchen. As irrational as it was, especially since we planned on all three of us sticking together for warmth—jealousy flashed through me at the decision.

When Adam pulled candles from one of the boxes he had stacked against the wall, the feeling surged again. He extracted several colorful, soy candles, and set them around the room.

"Pretty colors," Brooke said as Adam lit each one. "Will the scents clash?"

He shook his head. "They're unscented."

"Oh." Brooke sounded like she'd never heard of such a thing.

I suspected she didn't know what the candles were really for, but I recognized them as one of Adam's favorite *special occasion* toys. Wax play meant pain plus art, and of course he enjoyed that. I'd enjoyed being the recipient on occasion as well, but now I was wondering how Brooke would react.

It didn't matter, because we were using the candles to light the room. Nothing more.

I lit a fire in the stove and made sure the smoke was going up the chimney instead of into the house, and Adam got Brooke situated in bed. I returned to find her in a half-reclined position with her leg propped up on a few pillows.

A chill had already settled into the house, so Adam and I made ourselves comfortable on either side of Brooke and pulled the comforter around us. We were all fully clothed, so it wasn't the sexiest thing I'd ever done, but it sent a thrill racing through me anyway.

"Since it's too early for bed, what should we do?" Adam asked.

I had a few ideas, but I wasn't sure getting naked and sticky was the smartest way to kick off an evening without power or heat. We'd save that until the lights came back on.

"What's Sebastian's deal, do you know?" Brooke asked. "How do you go from EMT to new age tea shop owner?"

When it came to the history of this street, I had a pretty solid base of knowledge. Though my grandparents left out the basement details from the stories they told me as a kid, I assumed the rest of what they told me had some elements of truth in them, and I'd seen how the place changed since then. I also knew the stories of most of the people on the street.

And Sebastian's story was one of the most interesting ones. "He's a genius. That's not a phrase I toss out there lightly, he's one of those high IQ people. His senior year of high school, he came up with a killer tech idea. Well, killer at the time. He was going to build a website that made it easy to book flight, hotel, and car rentals, basically reserve your entire vacation, in a single place."

"Did someone steal his idea?" Brooke sounded fascinated.

I winced. "Not exactly."

"Sebastian is a big idea guy. Big ideas, but the way he wants to put those ideas into practice aren't always the most marketable. Not that I take issue with that." Creation for the sake of creation was a wonderful thing. "But he had a friend at the time who saw a different application for Sebastian's idea. He didn't share that insight with Sebastian, but he did sell the concept to investors. Hundreds of millions in investments, for a piece of software that was nothing like what Sebastian was building."

Adam hissed. "Ouch. Why don't I know this story?"

"It's not exactly the kind of thing he broadcasts." Though I wasn't sure why *I'd* never told Adam. "Anyway, like so many vaporware products of the early 2000's, the company crumbled when investors realized there was nothing there. Sebastian was so burned on the whole thing that he got out of tech completely, and got his EMT certification instead. He was doing that until his grandmother passed away about six years ago and left him her shop. He feels an obligation to make it work."

We made our way down the street, story-wise, talking about Aubrey and her place, the music shop, and every other building, business, or owner I knew the history of. Brooke and Adam both seemed to devour the stories.

"What about you?" Brooke's question surprised me.

It shouldn't have—it made sense given the topic—but I stumbled on my response. "What about me?"

"What's Deacon's story?" she asked.

Adam raised his hand. "I would also like to know that."

"You already know my story. I basically grew up in this place and I inherited it. Except unlike Sebastian, I was familiar with my trade and happy to step into the role."

Brooke furrowed her brows and nodded her head. Her *hmm* was contemplative. "I give it a six."

"You're being generous. I might have gone with four-point-five rounded up to five," Adam said.

I turned enough to stare at both of them in disbelief, pretending I didn't get the reference. "Come again?"

Adam snorted. "That's what she said."

"I didn't have to. It happened regardless." Brooke blushed. "But *anyway*, your story. It's got good structure. Probably a decent narrator voice, though it didn't last long enough to be sure. It's plausible, but light on details and world-building. I give it a six."

I pushed out a growl. "We can't all have tragic backstories." Sure, there was more to my being here than what I'd offered, but it wasn't Pulitzer winning stuff, or whatever kinds of awards they gave for people talking about their pasts. Besides, summoning some of those memories left an ache inside that I would rather not dive into.

"Do you have any backstory?" Adam asked. "Baby Deacon just appeared out of nowhere one day and *bam* he was a smooth as fuck, all around great guy who knew everything about antiques and was destined for the shop he grew up in?"

Not quite. "Close enough." My story drew some parallels to Adam's, but I still wasn't in the mood to dive into it.

"Come on, you know my tale. You know Brooke's." Adam's voice was cajoling.

The past hammered in my skull, roaring to be released from the box it sat locked in ninety-nine percent of the time. "And I'm grateful that you trusted me enough to share."

"Tit-for-tat," Adam said. "At least a hint."

"*Drop it.*" The words came out harsher than I intended.

Adam clamped his jaw shut, and shock splashed across Brooke's face. I breathed deeply through my nostrils, clawing to lock away the memories again.

16

brooke

I WANTED to hear Deacon's story, but it was impossible to miss the edge in his voice.

"It's late. We should get some sleep." Deacon's tone flattened and he stood.

"I'll go sleep on the couch." Adam started to climb from the bed.

Just because they were younger than me didn't mean they could act like children. I grabbed Adam's wrist and gripped tight. "It's going to get cold in here tonight, and that's why we're all in here to begin with. We all just had sex a few hours ago, so it's not like we haven't gotten up close and personal with each other. Get your butts back in the bed."

"Kind of sexy when you say it like that." Adam settled in next to me again.

Deacon stayed as well. "We're supposed to keep an eye on you after all."

"Better."

The silence that settled in was a billion times more awkward than being naked on all fours in front of two men had been. I searched my brain for something neutral to try to get them talking again. *Oh.* "What are the candles for?" I had a nagging suspicion in the back of my mind thanks to a conversation with Carly, but I didn't want to assume.

"Lighting the room," Deacon said.

"Looking pretty," Adam added.

That couldn't be the entire answer. Not with the look they shared when Adam pulled the candles out. "So Adam has a full stash of gorgeous unscented candles, an entire rainbow, that he just happens to keep hidden away?"

Adam's smirk was telling. "I was a good Boy Scout."

"I like a man in uniform." Deacon leaned forward to look Adam over. "Probably not that one, but…"

This was so much better than the tension a few minutes ago. "Now tell me the real reason."

The men exchanged looks, and Deacon shook his head with a faint frown.

Like I wasn't going to notice? I gave my full attention to Adam—they were his candles, after all, and he seemed more likely to open up about almost anything than Deacon.

His smile was endearingly sheepish. "Yeah, yeah. Not like I can tell you *no*." He picked up one of the candles. "Hold out your arm, with the inside facing up."

I was far too curious to do anything but comply.

He grabbed my wrist with his free hand, his grip tight. The instant he tipped the candle, my impulse was to jerk out of his touch, but fascination won out. He drizzled hot wax in a lazy serpentine along my skin.

I sucked in a sharp breath through my teeth at the burn, but the pain wasn't as intense as I expected. It was also kind of hot in other ways. The kind of ways that coiled in my belly and traveled lower.

He let me go, and I twisted my arm this way and that, examining the simple but lovely pattern. "This is what they're for? It's pretty."

"Once you're stripped down"—Adam set the candle down—"they're for covering your body with artwork."

When Carly had explained wax play, it didn't sound so great, but the way Adam watched me, and the lingering sting on my skin made a pulse throb between my thighs. "So, it's a sex thing?" I asked.

Adam brushed my hair from my check and hovered his mouth near my ear. His hot breath brushed my cheek. "You tell me. Do you think you could get off after something like that?"

"Maybe." With the shivers of anticipation spilling through me, I wondered if I could get off just thinking about it.

"Do you want to try?" Deacon asked.

"So very much." I snapped my jaw shut. Did I just say that out loud?

Adam smirked. "After the power's back on, and we have control over things like the temperature of the running water." He peeled away the wax, leaving a faint red mark on my skin, but no real damage.

Deacon pressed his lips softly to the faint burn. "It looked like it needed kissing better."

"I think I need more of that. Kissing my boo boos better." When did I get this kind of bold? What had these men done to me?

Deacon looked contemplative. "You did just sprain your ankle."

"And as we've already discussed, we are supposed to take care of you," Adam said.

"But you're supposed to keep your ankle elevated, and we probably shouldn't get too naked. What with the cold and all." Deacon gestured vaguely.

Adam rested his palm on my cheek and turned my face to his. "Lucky for you, we're good at improvising."

His kiss went from a gentle mouth on mine to hard in an instant. He nipped my lips and swallowed my groans and kissed a hungry path along my jaw and down my neck, sucking on the soft skin as he went. The way he yanked my hair when he slid his hand to the back of my head and tightened his grip was delicious.

This must be what it felt like to be claimed.

Deacon shoved my sweater up, catching my bra on the way and pushing it over my breasts.

"I don't think those need to be kissed better," I teased.

He pressed his lips to the shell of my ear. "Best to not take any chances."

I couldn't argue that, especially with the heat of his palms on my skin and the delicious sting when he rolled my nipples between his fingers.

Adam undid my jeans with an efficiency I wasn't sure I'd mastered, and slipped his hand under the denim and over the cotton of my panties. He pressed in enough to entice and make me squirm while he sucked on the sensitive skin where my shoulder met my neck.

I couldn't remember the last time I'd had a hickey, but that hardly seemed to matter right now. Especially the way their attention had me squirming and clenching my thighs together.

"I want to taste you," Adam murmured against my shoulder.

I liked the way he said it, but I wasn't sure where he'd go from here. "You've had your mouth all over me."

"Not all over." He pressed his fingers harder against my panties above my opening.

A rush of anticipation flooded me as his meaning, and stupid logic followed on its heels. "I haven't showered or anything since before..."

Adam moved his mouth back to mine, his lips hovering millimeters from my skin. "I don't care." His whisper—his meaning—was as tantalizing as his touch.

Deacon kept up a light session of pinching and kissing while Adam helped me slide out of my bottoms. Adam was gentle every step of the way, making sure not to jar my foot or even disturb the bandage.

And then he was kissing up the inside of my thigh. When he dragged his tongue over my slick skin, I jerked into the incredible sensation. I lost track of where one lick ended and the next started, and when he slid a finger inside me, I was pretty sure I cried out

Deacon moved his mouth to my breasts, and sucking replaced pinching.

There were so many points of contact, it was as if a cord ran from each touch, all to a central point behind the throbbing button Adam was licking like a Tootsie Roll pop.

I fisted the sheets, needing something to ground myself. It didn't matter. Pleasure spilled through me, pushing me into orgasm and tearing ecstasy from my throat.

When they finally eased off, I sank into the bed, panting.

Deacon leaned past my shoulder and Adam raised his head, and they crushed their mouths together, my juices still glistening on Adam's face.

Hot. Holy Hellfire, that was scorching even.

And it made me wonder, "What would the two of you be doing if I wasn't here?"

"Sleeping," Deacon said.

Adam pouted. "Not giving you kisses to help you feel better."

"What he said." Deacon pointed at him. "His answer is way better than mine."

I laughed through my short breath. This was enticing and sexy and the orgasms... *wow*. And it was fun, too. "What if I wasn't here and the two of you were"—I hesitated, then felt dumb for letting such a simple word stall me given Adam just had his face up close and personal with my vagina—"horny."

Adam furrowed his brow. "So in this fictional scenario of yours, we both want to get off," he pointed at Deacon and then himself, "But you're nowhere to be found."

"That's the question, yes."

Deacon stood, strolled to the other side of the bed, gripped Adam's shirt and kissed him hard.

Their groans were delicious. I'd turned down Carly's MM books in the past because the thrill for me was imagining myself in the woman's place in any story, but watching this was a brand new level of yum.

I swore I could see the sparks between them and feel the pent-up frustration wrapping around them as it was released. The way one of them would shift his weight to take control of the kiss, then the other would turn to biting, each of them one-upping the exchange, was a distinct power struggle. But passion and need lay under it all.

It was all just. So. Hot.

And then they were both standing, shoving clothes out of the way without undressing. Shirts went up and pants hung off hips and the temperature in the room cranked up several degrees.

Was I allowed to touch myself while I watched them? I hoped so, because I was going to.

17

deacon

I NEEDED to lose myself in the physical—in Adam's rough touch and Brooke's soft sighs—and not lose myself in a jumble of thoughts from the past that tried to shove their way into my mind.

I dug my fingers into Adam's arms and gripped just as tightly to images of him going down on Brooke. The way she tasted on his lips after. The fact that she was going home in the morning and probably putting an end to lessons soon.

Nope. I wasn't dwelling on that last one.

The only thing that mattered right now was how hard I was. The sting that tugged my cock every time Adam bit me. His hand wrapped around my shaft as he jerked hard and fast. His grip was almost too much. *Almost.*

And the sounds Brooke made as she watched us. Seeing her dip her fingers into her pussy, her gaze never straying. She was stunning. Intoxicating.

Adam stroked me until I was grunting. Until I fucked his hand with heady desperation, wondering if I should pull away, but needing more at the same time.

Desire built inside, tightening in my balls. My eyelids fluttered, stars dancing in my vision, and my world swam. I came hard, jerking against Adam's touch, covering his hand and my jeans in a sticky white mess. My legs wobbled from the exertion. From the release.

I didn't have to worry about standing when Adam pushed me to my knees. I dragged his zipper down with my teeth, and Brooke's giggle-groan was pure delight.

Adam fisted his cock and pressed the head roughly to my lips, and I took him into my mouth. No one else could do this to me besides him. No one else turned me on by taking the lead. I was the one in control.

Unless I was with Adam.

He fucked my face, pushing deep, grunting as hard as he thrust.

I licked and sucked and fingered his sac, falling into the heady sensation of post-orgasm bliss combined with knowing how much he was enjoying this. I was barely aware of the sounds he made becoming harder. More punctuated. I was lost in the way he tightened his grip on the short strands of my hair.

Brooke let out a series of loud gasps that told me

she was coming again. *Fuck* I liked that sound, and after this, it would haunt my most vivid dreams.

When the first salty spurt from Adam hit the back of my mouth, I swallowed greedily, letting him spill down my throat until he was spent.

As he slid from my mouth, he sank onto the edge of the bed with a low groan and I sank back on my heels.

Silence rang loudly in the room, amplified by the still from outside. The flicker of candles and the occasional crack of flame from the other room added to the almost otherworldly feeling around us.

Maybe *this* was a vivid dream. It almost felt like one. Potent and alluring and the kind of thing that would suck me in and keep me here until I didn't want anything else.

I shook the thought aside and stood abruptly. "I need a change of clothes. I'll bring you something too, Brooke."

"I'll figure out the best way to clean us up." Adam stood, spun, and kissed Brooke on the forehead. "Don't move."

She raised her brows, and I nearly choked on the envy as I swallowed it back.

Adam and I left and returned about the same time. His faint smirk was hard to miss when he pressed a washcloth to Brooke's skin and she squealed.

"It's cold." She laughed.

"No hot water." Adam shrugged. "We'll keep you warm, I promise."

When he was done. I helped Brooke slide into a pair of my sweats, and the three of us were soon cuddled together under the blanket again.

"What did you think of tonight's bonus lesson?" I barely hid my wince as the question passed my lips. It tasted like a foul thing to ask, but I needed to cement for myself what I was doing here.

Brooke's expression flickered, but returned to neutral in a blink, but Adam's scowl stayed fixed in place.

"It was good. Thank you." Brooke sounded like she was taking about dinner and not sex.

I wanted to take back the words and explain.

That was post coital bliss doing the thinking for me. A good night's sleep, and I'd be fine in the morning.

I WASN'T SURPRISED to find Adam and Brooke gone the next morning, but it was nice hearing their voices drift into the bedroom. Nicer even than hearing the sizzle of the radiator and feeling the heat in the room. Power was back on.

I wandered into the kitchen to find Brooke in one chair with her foot propped up on another, and Adam making breakfast. It was so normal and domestic and heartwarming and I refused to let it lull me into any false sense of belief that what was going on with me and them was anything other than sex and friendship.

We exchanged generic *good morning* greetings while I grabbed some coffee and took a seat across from Brooke at the table.

"Power's hooked up in the basement," she said. "You're free to do whatever you need down there."

"You shouldn't have gone down there." My retort came out as more of a grumble.

She scowled. "You're welcome."

"I tried to tell her *no*." Adam set a plate in front of me with pancakes and eggs. "She's very persuasive when she wants to be."

Images flashed in my mind of all the ways Brooke could *persuade* Adam, and I clenched my jaw.

Brooke started to stand, and Adam nudged her back into her seat. He took her empty plate to the sink and rinsed it.

This was too sweet. Too wrong.

"I was careful and he was the perfect escort." A soft smile played on Brooke's face.

Jealousy surged inside, and I swallowed it. Did I wake up on the wrong fucking side of the bed or what?

Adam joined us at the table, his own coffee in hand. "Roads are plowed. I'm going to take Brooke to the clinic so they can check out her ankle, then drop her off at home."

Brooke should stay here. I squashed the impulse to spit out the words. To follow them with *We'll take care of you.* She needed to go home to her actual family. " Sounds good."

"So, thank you for last night. All of it." Brooke's voice grew softer.

I gave her a smile that didn't feel real on any level. "Of course. What are friends for?"

That seemed to be enough to kill the breakfast conversation. A short while later, Adam helped Brooke downstairs, and they were on their way.

My pancakes tasted like sawdust. Weird, because Adam was usually a great cook. I cleaned up after myself and headed down to the shop to work. Both of my employees had called in, due to bad weather conditions, but I didn't expect many customers, for the same reason, so it wasn't a big deal.

I returned a few calls about the furniture people saw on Adam's channel, and since I had to keep an eye on the shop, I settled in to wait.

When the *Adam's Family* chime rang through the store, I stood. The *interested* look I adopted faded to a scowl when I saw Travis strolling toward me. "What can I do for you?" I clipped off the words.

"I heard you've been doing some electrical wiring in a basement you aren't supposed to have."

I wasn't going to take any chances with the nuance in his words. "*I* wasn't. I had a licensed electrician do it. And since the basement is original to the building, I can't *unhave* it."

"If by licensed, you mean Brooke, is her work the reason the power went out on the whole block last night?"

I clenched my fists as suppressed frustration from

this morning rushed back in the form of fury. Could I get away with it if I threw a punch? "The power went out because the transformer blew. Same one that dies in a noisy *bang* every six months or so. Brooke is more competent at her work than anyone I know. Get out or I'll make you."

"I didn't say what I came to say."

"I don't care." Maybe I should—he had a lot of say about what happened to this block—but fuck him. "This is still my shop and still private property. If you want to tell me something, send an email."

Travis shrugged. "Probably safer for me anyway, but you'll wish you heard me out when you read it." He turned and walked toward the door.

Adam was coming back as he was leaving, and jarred Travis with his shoulder on the way past.

Childish? Without question. Did I laugh anyway? Without question.

"What's The Tool want?" Adam asked when he reached the counter.

"Don't know, don't care. How's Brooke?"

"She has to stay off her feet for at least two weeks and she's not happy about it." Adam didn't look happy either.

I was disappointed, but this was as good a time as any to remind myself of the rules I'd set on our relationship. Brooke was a friend I was giving lessons to. If the teacher couldn't practice what he preached, what good was he as a teacher? "She has to do what she has to do."

A frown whispered across Adam's face.

"We should check with some other people on the block, see if they can help us while she's out of commission," I said.

"Good idea." This time Adam's frown lingered. "Brooke did say—more than once—that we should visit and keep her updated, so she didn't get lonely."

I wasn't sure that was smart, but if we weren't having sex, I'd go see her as a friend. "Okay."

Adam's sigh almost sounded like a growl.

I wasn't going to ask why, because I wasn't sure I had a retort to whatever was bothering him. "Do you mind working today?" I asked instead. "I want to do a full inventory of the basement, now that we have power."

Adam's *sure* was as unenthusiastic as anything I'd ever heard, but he settled onto the stool behind the register.

I headed into the basement. A light switch sat at the bottom of the stairs, and when I flicked it, the entire space lit up. Brooke was good. I spent the next several hours cataloging everything, moving as much of it as I could into some semblance of order while I worked.

Was antique sex furniture subject to the same zoning laws as adult toys? There was what we'd told Travis, and then there was the reality and I had no idea if I could actually sell this stuff. I hoped so.

My phone chimed with a new email from Travis, and I ignored it.

About fifteen minutes later a text from Aubrey came through. *What the fuck is he thinking?*

This couldn't be good.

It was followed quickly by one from Adam. *You should get up here.*

Nope. Not good at all.

I made my way back to the main shop, to find that Aubrey, Sebastian, and others from the block had gathered around the counter by Adam. They were all talking over each other and the general tone in the room felt like panic mixed with fury.

Maybe I should've read the message from Travis. "What's going on?"

"Mr. Paddock"—Sebastian said Travis name with poisonous disdain—"is pushing through zoning regulations about wiring. That all of the buildings have to be brought up to modern code."

"He can't do that." I should know by now that Travis could do a lot more than seemed legal. He had too many connections to the people with money and who made the decisions.

Aubrey scowled. "Well guess what. He is."

18
adam

IT HAD ONLY BEEN a few days since Brooke stopped by, barely more than a weekend, but her absence was tangible. I filled some of the time by filming Sebastian's shop and posting the video.

A few friends on the street were happy to help us finish the basement build-out, but scheduling difficulties meant that wasn't happening for another week. We'd decided to make it an anti-Valentine's Sunday, the day before the holiday.

By Tuesday afternoon, I was fidgety and looking for something new to fill my time. Deacon and I were sitting in the back room of the shop, having finished getting video of most of the furniture in his basement.

"We should visit Brooke." The words popped out of my mouth before I registered what they meant.

Deacon looked surprised. "And do what?"

"Say *hi*. See if she needs anything. Hang out for a bit."

"She'd call if she needed anything. Or send one of her kids. And when in the history of ever have we just *hung out?*"

That didn't mean we couldn't start. "Dylan is working. Dean will be in in an hour to help. Let's go."

"Dean is coming in because I have a lot to do." Deacon waved me off. "Admin shit. If you want to go, I'm not stopping you."

But Brooke is your *friend*. The odd protest lodged in my brain. I saw her as at least a friend at this point, and as much as I tried not to, I was hoping for more than that. "Fine. Go do your *admin shit*. I'll see you later."

Deacon scowled, but he didn't stop me.

As I walked to my car, I called Brooke. When she answered, her voice made me smile, even saying something as simple as *hello*.

"Hey. You busy?" I asked.

"Super, super busy. I'm training for a marathon, and after that I thought I'd go rock climbing." Her reply was playful.

"That sounds super fun. But how about instead I bring over some pizza and keep you company while you *don't* do those things."

"You expect me to drop my busy afternoon for you?"

"And pizza. Extra sausage."

Brooke laughed. "I don't know if that's innuendo or if you're serious."

"I never joke about pizza. As for the sausage… All depends on how the day goes."

"I'd love some company. The pizza sounds good too, but isn't necessary."

"I'll be there in less than thirty." As I disconnected and climbed into my car, I was grinning. How did such a simple exchange brighten my day this way?

When I got to Brooke's, pizza in hand, a goofy giddiness was racing through me. I felt like a teenager on a first date.

In some ways, the anticipation felt wrong. I'd watched Deacon lust after her for years, but never act on it. He'd made it more than clear that he didn't intend to—not at a romantic level—so was there really an issue with me seeing if Brooke was interested?

I had no idea. Were there rules in a case like this? Did I care?

I rang the bell, and it chirped in response.

"Come on in." Brooke's voice seemed to filter from nowhere.

I pushed inside the house to find her on the couch, her foot propped up on pillows and her phone in hand.

"New doorbell?" I asked.

"Paige and Bryan decided I needed a remote control one with a camera, if I was going to be home alone and immobile for two weeks."

That was cool. "Super smart."

"Especially since they've been asking to install one

for a while now, and this gave them the excuse they needed." Brooke scooted into a sitting position.

I moved the pillows under her leg to rest at her new spot. "I would've taken the chance too if I were them."

She shook her head. "Don't tell them that. If I let them have their way, my entire house would be *smart*. I don't need my fridge to know more about its contents than I do."

"A problem easily solved by storing nothing but condiments, beer, and enough milk for cereal and coffee. Do you want this now or later?" I held up the pizza box.

"You're such a bachelor," Brooke teased. "Or rather, you put up a good front. I know what the contents of Deacon's fridge were pre- and post-Adam. And I would love some pizza now. I don't know if it's good or bad that Paige hasn't built me a robot yet to make me lunch."

"You don't need a robot, you've got me. Multipurpose, I don't need batteries, and I vibrate at infinite frequencies."

Brooke's laugh was light. "I'll have to try out some other settings when I'm up to it."

Fuck yes she would. "Don't go anywhere."

She raised her brows.

I vanished into the kitchen long enough to find plates and grab us each a few slices of pizza. "I really am happy to bring you lunch every day," I said when I returned to the living room.

"I'm not sure if that's innuendo or not." She took a plate from me.

I sat on the couch near her feet. "It wasn't, but only because I need you to recover as quickly as possible, so it can be." Reservations or not, apparently I was all-in on this flirting-with-Brooke thing.

And the pink on her cheeks that colored her smile implied she didn't mind. "I'm going to have a hard time turning down an offer like that."

"Then it's a date. Or a dozen of them." I grinned.

We spent the afternoon talking, until her kids got home from school.

"Ooh, did you come over to help me with my bike?" Paige asked.

I glanced at Brooke.

"He came over to bring me pizza," she said.

Bryan huffed. "And we had to eat school food?"

"You were excited this morning that it was Taco Tuesday. *We don't need extra money for lunch, Mom.*" Brooke's voice deepened in what I assumed was a Bryan impersonation. "*We'll have tacos for lunch, Mom.*"

Paige rolled her eyes. "That you think for even a moment that school lunch tacos are on the same level as Gia's Deep Dish makes me wonder if you're the same woman who raised us."

"There are leftovers in the fridge." I gestured toward the kitchen, then glanced at Brooke. "Unless that's going to ruin their dinner?" I didn't want to step on any toes.

Brooke twisted her mouth. "I'm not sure if you remember being seventeen, but it takes a lot more than a slice or two of pizza to ruin their appetites."

Her kids cheered, vanished into the kitchen, and returned before Brooke and I could restart our conversation.

"Okay, we're stealing Adam now." Paige took a bite out of the slice in her hand.

"Only if Adam agrees, and don't you want to heat that up first?" Brooke asked.

Bryan shook his head. "Takes too long."

I gave Brooke's good leg a gentle squeeze. "I did promise to help Paige with her bike. I'll be back."

"Remember he's doing you a favor. Be nice." Brooke looked at her kids.

Bryan snorted. "We're always angels, just like our mom raised us to be."

Brooke rolled her eyes and waved us outside.

I followed Paige and Bryan, but instead of steering us toward the garage where I thought she did most of her work, they led me to a barn behind the house.

"It's my understanding this place is off limits." I did *not* want to be put in the position of *to narc or not to narc.*

"Pft." Bryan glanced over his shoulder at me. "Because Mom is afraid of creepy crawlies."

"And barns falling on her kids." Look at me, being an adult and shit.

Paige stopped a few feet from the doors. "The barn is structurally sound, but before we show you what's inside, you have to promise, swear on your fucking life, to not tell Mom."

"No can do." I shook my head.

Paige sighed. "What if I promise you first that it's not illegal or dangerous? Please? It's a surprise. We will tell Mom, just not until it's done."

How was I supposed to be the wet blanket over a surprise? "My definition might be different than yours. But as long as it's not going to get anyone hurt or arrested, I won't tell."

"Okay." Paige and Bryan opened the doors enough to let us in, then closed them behind us, encasing us in darkness. "Light," she said.

A series of bright, bare bulbs flickered on a few feet away, temporarily blinding me. When I blinked away the brightness, I was looking at a tarp over something large. But it was a new tarp, not something that had been sitting back here for decades, and tools were set up on stands around it.

Paige grabbed one side of the tarp and Bryan the other.

"Are you ready for this?" he asked. "You're not ready, but do you think you're ready?"

He was right—I didn't know if I was ready. "Sure."

They yanked the tarp away to reveal a small, World War I tank. "Holy shit." I recognized it instantly, because there was an ancient photograph of it tucked away in Deacon's shop, with the old owner standing proudly next to it. "Pretty sure *tank* falls under the category of *could kill you*. Why do you have a tank?"

"It came with the house," Paige said.

Bryan nodded. "And it's only going to kill you if you put ammo in it. It's not really big enough to run things over."

"No more than Deacon's truck," Paige added.

It was a *small* tank, all things considered. "What are you doing with it? And what about your bike, Paige?"

She ducked her head. "My bike is fine. It was a ruse to get you back here. We need an adult for some things, and also some knowledge I don't have."

"I don't know anything about tanks except that they go *boom*."

"But you've got an instinct for it, like Paige does," Bryan said.

Page handed me a clipboard. "I'm fixing it up for a final grade in one of my classes, and I'm going to use it to get an apprenticeship after I graduate. You have to keep it a secret and help us. *Please*."

How was I supposed to refuse an offer like that? I was about to work on a fucking tank. "All right. I'm in."

We spent the next few hours going through what they'd already done and figuring out what next steps were. When Brooke texted Paige to remind her it was her turn to make dinner, we had a good idea of where we were going next.

"You should stay for dinner," Bryan said as we headed toward the house.

I wished I could. Was that crossing a line? "I'm working at Deacon's tonight. I need to get back."

Both teenagers frowned. "Okay, but come back tomorrow."

The next few days went a lot the same—I'd stop by with lunch, spend time talking to Brooke, then go help Paige and Bryan in the barn after school. Wednesday, Brooke's feet were in my lap instead of a pile of cushions between us, and by Friday, I was sitting behind her, propping her up, tempted to pull her into my lap.

Fuck it.

I gripped her chin to tilt her face to mine, and brushed my lips over hers. The air sparked between us, ignited by her gasp fading to a sigh.

She twisted her body, turning toward me and kneeling without breaking the kiss.

This was soothing chaos—calming my soul but making my pulse race—and I needed more. I slid my hand to the back of her neck, gripping tight and holding her captive. Licking along the seam of her lips then thrusting my tongue into her mouth. Swallowing her moans. Devouring her.

It was tempting to completely let go of my restraint and push into things hard and fast, but there was pain for pleasure and then there was re-injuring her ankle so she was stuck like this even longer. I didn't want any version of the second option.

Brooke traced along my chest, teasing with a light touch as she outlined each contour she came to.

Dude. Deacon's voice barked in my thoughts, jarring me out of the moment. As I leaned back, reality rushed in around us, putting up an invisible barrier.

"What's wrong?" Brooke asked.

I was hard as a rock, I wanted desperately to pin her on her back and fuck her until she screamed with pleasure, and I had a two second loop of Deacon interrupting stuck in my mind. "I can't."

"Can't what? Kiss me? You were doing an incredible job." Hurt slid into Brooke's voice.

"I just... Deacon—"

"Isn't here. He has nothing to do with this."

But didn't he? Something told me that wasn't the right thing to ask.

Brooke scowled and scooted away. "He's made it crystal clear how he sees his relationship with both of us. I was never *with* him and supposedly neither were you. Anything that happens between you and me should be between you and me."

On the one hand she had a good point, but...

"Or is this bros before hoes?" Brooke spat out the question.

"No." At least I knew that answer. "That's not... You're not... *No.*"

She scrubbed her face. "I think you should go."

"Because I won't make out with you?" Stupid, Adam. Stupid. Stupid.

Brooke growled. "Because our invisible friend's presence is apparently more potent than whatever we were just doing."

If I took it back, I could stay. We could talk. More.

And I'd feel guilty. "I'll be back tomorrow with lunch."

"No. It's Saturday. I've got things covered. You don't need to come back next week, either."

"Right." I walked out of the farmhouse. The conversation played on repeat in my mind the whole drive back to Deacon's, but I wasn't any closer to knowing what the right choice was when I arrived.

19
brooke

I WAS STILL TRYING to process what happened with Adam when the twins got home.

"Are you the only one here?" Bryan asked when they walked in the front door.

Your mother made a bad judgment call and now your friend isn't coming back. I'd have to work on that answer. "You were expecting someone else?"

"Adam," Paige said. "To help us."

Three days and he was part of their lives. I should be grateful I'd never tried to date before now. Not that Adam and I ever made it to the dating. This was so messed up. "Maybe next week."

They both shrugged, made sure I was set, and then they were off doing their own thing again.

I felt like I should be able to shrug things off as easily as they just had, but here I was asking myself if it was me.

I shrugged off the cloud enough to give my family

my attention through the evening and into the next day, but the self-doubt and questions lingered in the back of my mind.

Saturday was the day of the high school Sweetheart's dance. As noon crept up and then rushed past, I felt an empty pit in my chest at the realization I wouldn't have Adam's company today.

Or Deacon's, since he seemed to have dropped off the face of the earth since I hurt my ankle.

Fortunately, distractions were on the way. Carly arrived a little after two, to help Paige and Jamie with their hair, and Daria came with her so we could all hang out and ooh and ahh over my babies going to one of their last dances before they graduated.

Bryan grumped around the house through most of the makeover process, grumbling about *girls*, but as soon as Aubrey showed up with their outfits, to make sure the three of them were all wearing things right, he was all over getting into his suit.

I wasn't sure if his excitement was about the suit or Aubrey. Hopefully it wasn't the latter—I wasn't prepared to deal with my teenage boy falling for a woman in her thirties.

While the kids were getting dressed and Carly and Daria were taking care of other things, Aubrey approached me. "Can I ask you something?" Her voice was quiet.

"Sure."

"You and Deacon…"

Oh. *Oh.* My answer lodged in my throat, carried

on the doubt of the last day. "We're just friends." I'd waited too long to say it—it didn't sound believable.

She fiddled with her watch, sliding it up and down her arm. "Are you sure?"

"Absolutely positive." I managed to sound convincing this time, and Deacon had driven home over and over how much *just friends* we were.

"I can't figure out the fringes." Paige flounced into the room, interrupting the conversation.

Aubrey moved away from me to help Paige, Jamie, and Bryan. She stayed on hand while I took a billion pictures, and left when the kids did.

"I'm looking forward to dress shopping with Alana when she's old enough for dances," Daria said. "But I am *not* looking forward to the drama and the boys."

Carly pulled three hard lemonades from the fridge. "Make your men deal with the boys."

Daria took a bottle from her and twisted off the top. "Tanner might invite them to watch movies with us."

"If Colin likes them, you know you're safe." I had a pretty high opinion of my younger brother. "Problem solved."

Daria snorted a laugh and helped me hobble back to the couch. "You're lucky yours are still angels at seventeen." She handed me my drink.

"They're not angels. They're smart little demons who are lovable enough to get away with it." Though, I really was lucky my kids were as good as they were.

"So are cats," Carly said. "I'd rather have the cats."

I took a sip of something that was distinctly lemon plus alcohol. Being raised religiously, I hadn't taken my first drink until I was in my thirties, and I didn't drink much now. But every once in a while, especially with friends I trusted, I liked to indulge a little. "You can't tell me you're not a little awed by seeing them in their dance clothes tonight."

"I won't deny that—they were adorable." Carly conceded. "The thing is—they're your problem at the end of the night, not mine."

Daria laughed. "You're so jaded."

"And you love me anyway, bitch. Enough about kids. I want to know what turned Brooke to the dark side." Carly looked at me.

I stared back, not comprehending. She wasn't talking about my *lessons* with Deacon and Adam, because no one knew about those. Unless it was actually obvious. Was there some sort of mark on me that said *I've gotten laid for the first time in more than a decade*? No. "The dark side?"

"Wanting more books with spanking. *Other things*, I believe is how you put it."

Daria leaned in, eyes wide. "*Really*. I thought you were content with keeping the details sparse and the sex vanilla."

Was I blushing? I had to be with how hot my face was. "I got curious."

"Just like that?" Carly asked.

"I might have had a little help." Was I allowed to talk about this? Both women were familiar with casual sex—I'd heard Carly's stories especially—so it didn't seem like they'd judge me. But this wasn't just my story.

Daria took a long swallow of her drink. "Spill. We need to know."

"You don't even have to share all the dirty details. Who is he? Did you get yourself a young stud or two like Daria has?" Carly set her bottle aside and leaned in, elbows on her knees.

I wasn't sure how comfortable I was hearing my brother as a *young stud*. "It's not like that."

"Not like what?" Daria prodded.

"I just have a friend or two helping me figure out what dating might be like." There. That was the truth. Mostly.

Daria made a *tsk* sound. "Which is why you're blushing furiously. You can't turn back now that you've opened up this forum of curiosity. We need information."

I really did want to share with *someone*. "So, Deacon is giving me lessons in casual sex, and Adam may have been there a time or two as well."

"A time or two implies more than two times. Wait. Deacon? With the..." Daria gestured at her arms.

I could guess what she meant. "The tattoos. Yes."

"Give me your hands." Carly held out both of hers.

We each did the same. She grabbed our wrists and licked our palms.

"The fuck?" Daria scrubbed her hand on her jeans.

I mimicked the gesture.

"The two of you obviously have some kind of *two men at once* mojo. I need me some of that," Carly said.

Except now I had *no men* mojo, because one of them didn't want more and the other was his best friend. Apparently there were different types of lonely, and sleeping with a man who only wanted sex was a type I didn't care for at all.

I shook the thought aside. "You're going back to Italy next month, aren't you?" I asked Carly.

She wrinkled her nose. "No. I had to push Italy back, but I might be hitting up Birmingham."

"You said Birmingham and not Buckingham, right? No castles in your near future?"

"Not for her." Daria shook her head. "But maybe a few gators."

We were still talking and joking a few hours later, when I heard a car in the driveway. It was too early for the kids to be back. Did I dare hope it was Adam? Would I send my friends away if it was? Screw that— he chose to walk out, he could come back to—

The door slammed open and Bryan stormed through. He headed straight for the stairs, and anger spilled from him.

Paige wasn't far behind. "It's not my fault. I didn't know." Her voice was raw.

Bryan slammed his bedroom door in response.

"Fuck you too." Paige screamed and stormed into her own room.

I sighed.

"What were you saying about demons?" Carly's voice was sympathetic.

"Do you want help? Can we do anything?" Daria asked.

I shook my head. "I've got this, but thank you."

But as Carly and Daria left, I wasn't sure that I had anything under control.

20
deacon

When Adam came back from Brooke's in a foul mood, I tried to ignore the ember of smugness inside. He wouldn't talk about what happened, which wasn't unusual. His refusal to smile was strange, though.

I wasn't going to push the issue.

Saturday he was in his room most of the day editing video of the furniture in the basement. I knew because he sent me clips every so often to check out and approve. Proof he was fine.

Sunday morning he was quiet, but the foul mood was gone as he and I got ready for some of our friends from the block to help us with prepping the basement to be usable as a sales floor. It was weird that Brooke wouldn't be here, and even more unusual that I hadn't seen her all week. Obviously I wouldn't, since she was staying off her feet, but I missed her company.

Which, of course I did—she was a good friend.

Sebastian brought pastries from the bakery down the street, with an apology from the owner for not being here. I didn't expect them to be. Sundays were huge for the bakery, even though most of the stores on the block were closed today.

Evie, who owned the hardware store, showed up with coffee. It was a universally accepted fact that she made the best coffee. Aubrey brought iced tea for later, which she stored in my fridge.

Sebastian wrinkled his nose when she told us what it was.

"Since when are you a tea snob?" Aubrey asked.

"Since I learned what real tea tasted like."

Evie made a sound like *pft*. "Give a guy a store and suddenly he's a fucking expert."

"*Yes.*" Sebastian's tone said *obviously*. "Like none of you know your shit?"

Adam cringed and stuck out his tongue. "Not personally. Gross, dude."

Evie made a gagging noise and Aubrey threw a pair of work gloves at him.

Adam was back to normal.

We snacked on pastries while Adam explained the plan for the day. Furniture would be pushed to the very middle of the room and covered. We'd buff out the stone floor and cover the wires Brooke put in place.

Something pinged in my chest at her name. Strange.

Evie and Adam got to work on making sure the

molding would cover the wiring, while Sebastian, Aubrey and I rearranged furniture.

Sebastian stepped away to take a call.

"How's Brooke doing?" Aubrey asked. "How's her ankle?"

What? "Weren't you over there yesterday?" There weren't a lot of secrets on Main Street. Besides, Aubrey told me a few days ago that she was helping Brooke's twins with their outfits for the dance.

Aubrey shrugged. "Oh. Yeah."

"You're being weird," I said.

Sebastian returned, and Aubrey didn't say anything.

"Aubrey?" I prodded.

"Nothing. I'm fine. Nothing."

Sebastian looked between us. "Did I interrupt? Do you want me to come back?"

"Would you?" Aubrey's voice was instantly playful.

I wasn't in the mood for, well, abrupt mood shifts. "Don't go." I grabbed Sebastian's arm. "I can talk about how much I want you while you're here."

"You couldn't handle me." Sebastian tugged away and went back to work.

I snorted. "Okay. Keep telling yourself that."

He sighed heavily and gazed at some point in the distance. "I have to." His tone was wistful. "It's the only way I can sleep in my big, lonely bed at night."

"Oh. Is Rachel out of commission again?" Aubrey asked sweetly.

Sebastian's pout was exaggerated. "I had to special order a puncture kit, because *Evie doesn't carry them.*" He raised his voice at the end of his statement.

"What?" Evie looked up from across the room. "If I don't carry it, you don't need it. Don't blame me because you poked one too many holes in your blow-up doll."

A glance around the room showed I wasn't the only one shocked she had the perfect response on hand.

"How did you know what they were talking about?" Adam asked.

"I'm psychic." Evie tossed out casually. "Or smart. Or a good guesser. Take your pick."

God, I loved this block.

We went back to work, Evie's router creating too much noise for much conversation. When Adam called for another set of hands to hang the next section of trim, Sebastian joined them.

Aubrey and I moved further away, out of everyone else's view, to move more furniture.

"You and Brooke... Have things changed between you?" Aubrey's soft question startled me.

Why? Did she say something? I shook the thought aside. "Nope. We're still good friends."

"You're sure."

"You've already asked her. What did she say?" I couldn't help it. I needed to know.

"Same thing."

I felt the answer like a stone in my chest, but what else was Brooke supposed to say? "See? Just friends."

"So what if you had a friend who wanted to be more?" Aubrey asked.

I stopped pushing the vanity I was moving. Would I go for it if Brooke wanted more? The thought didn't sit well with me. That meant admitting... No. It hurt too much to touch memories of families I almost had and then lost. "I don't know."

"What if I could help you figure it out?"

A woman's perspective could be helpful. "How?"

Aubrey draped her arms around my neck and pressed her body to mine.

What the hell?

She shifted her weight and her frame rubbed against mine. "Does this help?" she asked, her mouth close enough to mine I felt the question. She kissed me.

I was too stunned to do anything in return. This was so fucking awkward.

Aubrey let go and put several inches between us, her face a stone mask. "I guess that's a no."

"I don't feel that way about you." And I didn't think she felt that way about me. Seriously—what the hell?

"Of course you don't. I was just kidding." Her laugh was forced. "A joke between friends, right?" Her voice strained.

Shit. How did I never see this? "I'm sorry, Bree." I

should've known... But it wouldn't have changed how I felt.

"Totally good." Her reply was high and tight. "But I need to go. You don't need my help anyway—everything's under control." As she talked, she backed away. "See you all later," she called, before she ran up the stairs.

Shitshitshitshitshit.

"What did you do to her?" Adam asked.

"One too many sex doll jokes?" Evie offered.

"One too few clues," Sebastian said.

That was about right. I needed to make things right with Aubrey, but I doubted she wanted me pounding on her door right now telling her *I'm sorry I don't like you that way, but I don't want to lose your friendship*. This sucked.

When we called it a night, it was almost ten, and we'd finished more than half the basement. One more day and we'd be set.

Adam and I headed up to our apartment, and settled in front of the TV with pizza. He picked the movie, promising I would love it.

I usually did.

"So you and Brooke... You're just friends?" His tone was casual.

I had instant flashbacks to the conversation with Aubrey. "Yes. Why do people keep asking me that? Are you going to declare your undying love for me?"

"So that's what happened with Aubrey. Does she know the two of you have zero chemistry?"

"Apparently not." Why was I bothered that he didn't answer a question I asked in total jest?

"You have to make things right with her," Adam said.

No shit, Sherlock. "Why are you asking about Brooke?"

"Because I want more with her."

More. The word hit me hard before I finished processing what it meant, and tension cranked through me. I twisted my neck, but it didn't pop. "What if I say *no*?"

"You misunderstand." An edge sneaked into Adam's voice. "I'm not asking your permission. I'm telling you what's about to happen."

"But—"

"But what?" He was no longer friendly and casual. "You saw her first? You wanted her first? You've had so much time to figure out if you're going to make a move for Brooke, and then you finally did something. You could've had her before I even knew I was interested and she probably would've said *yes*. I mean, you got her to fuck you with no strings attached, so that's a good sign she's interested. But you keep fucking denying it."

I stared at Adam as he talked. Where the fuck did this come from, and why did his words dig deep?

"She's not a toy," Adam said. "You don't get to play with her when you want and put her on the shelf out of reach of anyone else when you're done. She's a fucking human being. One I'd like to get to know a *lot* better. That's all there is to it."

Any response I had stalled in the tight space in my lungs where an invisible fist had squeezed out all the air. What was I supposed to say to that, and why was I so furious at what sounded like reasonable logic?

21
brooke

THE TWINS STAYED in their rooms most of Sunday, and when they did emerge they managed to avoid each other and me.

Because I was going stir crazy and it was clear neither of them were going to cook, in the late afternoon I grabbed the cane Deacon had given me and used it to hobble around the kitchen. I suspected he and Adam would have a fit if they knew, but they weren't here.

The thought ached in my chest and my brain shouted back that I shouldn't care.

But I did. I missed their company. I missed what had been happening with Adam.

I shouldn't be missing the same from Deacon, but I did. Not that anything had been happening there.

I needed to not think about him. Instead, I made the twins' favorite—boxed mac and cheese mixed with a can of tortilla soup and crumbled up corn chips on top. It may not be gourmet, but it was easy and hopefully it would lure them out of their rooms.

Paige came down for dinner, but Bryan refused to.

She filled up her plate without a word and shoveled food into her mouth.

"You're both worrying me. You know that, don't you? Don't make me play the Mom Guilt Trip card." I ate more slowly.

She huffed and let her fork clatter to the table. "Please don't. I already have enough guilt for a lifetime."

That was a heavy burden to carry at seventeen. "Maybe telling me what happened will help with that?"

"I doubt it." She sighed heavily. "Bryan is upset with me because…" She huffed, and shoved more food into her mouth.

"Because why?" I kept my tone gentle. It was hard to imagine Paige doing anything to make her brother this mad.

"Because I guess he likes Jamie and he was going to tell her at the dance but apparently she likes me instead."

Oh. I was going to assume *like* meant more in both cases. Should I have been prepared for my kids' first huge fight to be over a shared love interest? "Okay." I voice my tone free of judgment.

"She kissed me, Mom. She fucking kissed me, and I don't know what I'm supposed to do about it." Paige sounded distraught.

"Do you like her?"

"She's my best friend, of course I do. But I like guys."

My experience with this was limited to when Colin came out, and that was decades ago, and he'd seemed so certain when he made the announcement. Did he deal with this kind of doubt before then? Not that it mattered now. I needed to reassure Paige and I didn't know how. "Can you tell her that?"

"But I liked the kiss."

Whatever I said next, I was going to fail. I just knew it. "Maybe you like girls too. Your uncle Colin—"

"This isn't about him. You don't understand." She pushed back from the table so hard her chair screeched against the tile, and she stomped from the room. "And don't you dare ask him to talk to me." Her screech from upstairs was laced with tears.

Damn it.

Monday morning Bryan left for school early with a friend, and Paige slunk out of the house soon after, refusing to talk to or even look at me.

And I was in for a day of staying off my feet. Carly had sent me more books, but reading them reminded me of a kind of passion I'd had so briefly and then lost. Both in the past and now, even though it was two different kinds of passion.

I missed Adam's company. I didn't know how to help my kids. I missed hanging out with Deacon.

Maybe TV would help distract me. It was rare for me to just sit and watch, especially during the day, but losing myself in someone else's drama might remind me that mine wasn't so bad.

Every commercial seemed intent on reminding me that today was Valentine's Day. That I should be celebrating love. That if I didn't get and give fancy presents, I wasn't loved. I'd been sans-Valentine for years. Why did the reminder hurt so much today?

Because I was having sex with a man who didn't want anything else. I wasn't supposed to be falling for him, but I might be. And at the same time I was absolutely enthralled with his best friend. For the first time in years I thought I might have more with someone...

I should've known better, but my heart ached regardless. The TV played in the background. Who were Harmony and Spencer? Where were Luke and Laura? How freaking old was I?

The doorbell rang and I grabbed my phone to see the cam. The sight of Adam standing on my front porch made my heart leap into my throat then plummet into my shoes. It was tempting to tell him to come in, but I didn't trust myself to not do something stupid once he was in here.

That didn't mean I could stand to send him away or stop watching him.

"I'm pretty sure you're in there," Adam said.

"And if you don't want to see me, I get it. But I'd really like to see you."

Me too. The reply lodged in my throat.

He held up two plastic bags. "I bought lunch and Valentine's Day gifts."

"You don't have to bring me presents in order to visit." I winced as the words slipped past my lips.

He smirked at the camera. "I know. I'm awesome all by myself."

I smiled in spite of myself. Letting him in would be so easy, and those words meant so much more than it seemed like on the surface. "What about Deacon?"

"What about him? You were right—this is about you and me."

I hovered my finger over the button that would unlock the door.

"Okay, I was prepared for this," Adam said. On my phone screen he set down the bags he was carrying, and pulled his phone from his pocket. A moment later, the tinny strains of *Careless Whisper* flitted through my door and phone speaker, half a second out of sync with each other.

"What are you doing?" I laughed.

"Boom boxing WHAM! outside your house, a la Deadpool."

How was I supposed to ignore a grand gesture like this? "I guess you can come in." The offer may have sounded casual but my heart was fluttering in my chest.

Adam strode through the front door, set everything on the table, and knelt on the floor next to where I sat on the couch. He cradled my face in his hands, searching my face. The way he pressed his lips to mine was tender enough it made my heart ache all over again, but an intensity flowed between us that stole my breath and made me want to linger here forever.

He pressed his lips to my forehead, then rested his forehead in the same spot against mine, never letting go of my face. "I don't know what this is, but I know I enjoy your company so much, and I want more of you. Let's see where this goes. Be my Valentine?"

Saying *yes* seemed like a big mistake.

Saying *no* wasn't an option, though. "Yes. I'd love to."

"Perfect." Adam stood. "Lunch first or dessert?"

"Dessert." That was my default answer when he was around.

He reached into one of the bags, and pulled out an egg carton. My curiosity turned to delight when he plucked out a large chocolate covered strawberry. "Open up." He pressed the sweet to my lips.

I tried to delicately bite into it, and the moment the chocolate hit my lips, I knew I'd failed. Bits of candy crumbled and juice dribbled down my chin. I squealed in surprise and failed to keep from making a mess.

Adam leaned in and licked my chin clean. I wasn't sure if I should giggle or moan.

We managed to make it through one strawberry,

but I was pretty sure we lost a quarter of the chocolate in the couch cushions. That was going to be a pain to clean up.

Not that I cared while Adam was running his mouth over mine and letting me suck his fingers clean.

We decided to save the rest of the dessert for later, though.

He settled next to me on the couch, and pulled me into his lap. How was this so easy?

"My first Valentine—" I snapped my jaw shut in horror as the words rushed past my lips. Was I really about to ruin this amazing moment by bringing up that part of my past? "Never mind."

"What's wrong?"

I shook my head. "You don't want to hear me talk about my deceased husband."

"Is it a good memory?"

I expected him to say *you're right* or change the subject or anything besides prodding for more. But the way Adam kept his hands wrapped loosely around my waist, and his casual tone, said he was genuinely interested.

"They're bittersweet," I said. "But there's an emphasis on the *sweet*."

Adam squeezed my hip. "I know you didn't pop into existence two weeks ago just for me. I won't be upset that you loved someone else as long as you don't expect me to be him."

I'd be more upset if Adam started acting like anyone other than himself. "I don't."

"Then tell me. Your first Valentine."

I nudged the edge of the memory, not sure I wanted to tug it loose. When the pain I expected didn't pulse in my heart, I dared unwrap the images. "He brought me daisies from the neighbor's yard, and drew me a comic strip of us going on a date."

"Was he an artist?"

Both of us had been discouraged from touching our more creative sides. That wasn't how people earned a living as adults. "Only casually. But he had a natural talent for it."

"He sounds like a good guy. Not that you'd love anyone who wasn't." Adam's tone was kind and sincere.

This was a bit surreal, but at the same time it was incredible. Sitting on the lap of a younger, gorgeous man, and talking about my husband as if it were the most natural subject.

"What about you? Do you have a good Valentine's Day story?" Was I sure I wanted to ask that? I may not be able to tug up the pleasantness as easily as Adam did, especially if he had some tale about an ex he'd had amazing, kinky, all-night sex with. The kind of evening I didn't even know enough about to imagine.

Though, my mind was trying.

"Today pretty much tops my list." Adam's words were sweet, but I wasn't sure I bought it.

"We made a mess eating fruit and now we're stuck on my couch because I have a twisted ankle."

He nuzzled my hair. "It's not the what, it's the who. Though, the what is pretty good too."

"And that's it? No other Valentine's Day compares?" Why was I pushing this?

"You don't want to hear about the other one."

Uncertainty clenched in my gut. Maybe he was right. "You just listened to me, of course I do. I already know you've been with other people," I said.

"But this story is about Deacon."

Oh. The man I shouldn't be missing. The one who didn't matter beyond being a casual friend, because I was cuddling with his best friend and enjoying the hell out of it.

Adam traced his thumb lightly along my skin, above the waistband of my sweats. "You can take the question back, if you'd like."

"I absolutely cannot. I'd like to know." Partly out of curiosity, and because it was polite to listen, and at least as much because I was more of a masochist than I realized. I needed to know more about how the two of them fit together.

Adam let out a laugh-sigh. "So, I'd lost my father about six months earlier, and my girlfriend walked away from me shortly after that because…" His whole body seemed to deflate beneath me when he sighed. "I didn't deal well with his passing."

"I'm sorry." I hated to hear his pain, and there had to be more than he was showing. "But we all deal with loss in our own ways. Who was she to judge?"

He shrugged. "We find out who people are when things are at their worst. But that's just backstory so you understand—Deacon was there for me. And that Valentine's Day he shut the shop early, cleared a huge space in the back room, and we spent the rest of the day watching ninja movies and monster movies that were so bad they were good. He told me the point was no calendar or person got to tell us when or what to feel."

"Which is why I would've been on your porch this morning, doing exactly what I did, regardless of if today was Valentine's Day or some random Wednesday in August," Adam said.

And that was about the sweetest story ever, tied up with the sweetest sentiment. "I'm glad you did. I'm glad you're here."

He pressed his lips to my forehead. "Me too."

We talked about so many little things. The kinds of conversation most people never wanted to overhear because it would be dry to anyone it didn't matter to, and we fed each other cheese and fruit for lunch. Adam's visit was simple but perfect.

He cleaned up after lunch, and pulled me back into his lap when he returned to the couch. I was going to have a hard time sitting anywhere else after this.

"You know what I've never done on Valentine's Day?" Adam said.

"Bungee jumping? Because I'm going to need to wait a little bit before we try that." I wiggled my injured leg.

He laughed, cupped my face, and gave me one of those long kisses that was as sweet as the strawberries had been, but had an underlying spice that made me think he might consume me in flame if he pushed a little harder.

He broke away and searched my face. "I've never made out with someone on Valentine's Day. You know, a really good, intense session of kissing and groping."

"It seems like a shame to not have experienced that at least once in your life." My imagination was already racing along the possibilities and my body whimpered for the reality of it.

"Right?" Adam slipped one hand to the back of my neck and tightened his grip, holding me captive. The way he crushed his mouth to mine was both playful and possessive, and I gasped in surprise.

An unwelcome voice came out of nowhere, whispering in the back of my mind and asking *what about Deacon?*

What about him? Adam was here, and I was enjoying every minute of his company, from the talking to the kisses and everything in between.

I pressed in harder, searing thoughts of only Adam into my mind, and memorizing the way his mouth seared my skin and consumed my soul and left me desperate for more.

22
adam

EVERYTHING ABOUT THIS WAS INCREDIBLE—BROOKE'S weight in my lap, the little sounds of delight she made, and the heat that flowed between us.

I felt like a teenager again, making out with my crush, and exploring each other like it was our first time. Her shirt was pushed up around her neck and her bra was undone, so I could memorize the topography of her breasts, and figure out which licks, sucks, and nibbles produced the best results.

She had my shirt off completely, and her nails on my skin were delicious.

The sound of tires on pavement and the growl of an engine reached us from outside and Brooke froze.

She was instantly as pale as her white cotton panties. "That's Paige's car."

And suddenly this was *way* too much like when I was a teenager. We managed to pull our clothes back on, straighten them, and slide Brooke back onto the couch just as the front door opened.

"Look, hon. Adam's back," Brooke said when Paige walked in.

Paige rolled her eyes. "Big fucking deal."

"Did I miss something?" I asked.

"Her best friend ki—"

"Oh my fuck." Paige talked over Brooke. "Are you going to tell everyone?" She turned from the room and a moment later a door slammed.

Brooke's sigh was nothing like the ones she was making just a few minutes ago. "There was a lot of that this weekend."

"Do you want me to talk to her?" Why did I just offer that? I didn't know anything about consoling teenagers, especially girls.

"You're sweet to offer, but I don't think she'd appreciate that. I should probably figure out how to get at least one of them talking to me again."

I hated to end the day on this note, but this seemed like a good reason to do so. "I had a lot of fun today."

"Me too." Brooke's smile was back. "Thank you."

"I'll be back tomorrow." And almost every day that she'd let me come back. I was addicted to this. I gave her one more long kiss, and stood. "Call me if you need anything?"

"I will."

As I was walking to my car, a horrible sound screeched out from the shed Brooke used as a workshop. It sounded like someone assaulting a robot. I followed the noise to find Paige beating on the gas tank of her motorcycle with a wrench.

"*Whoa*," I shouted over the noise. "What did the bike ever do to you?"

She scowled at me. "It won't start."

"I wouldn't either if you hit me repeatedly in the gut with a wrench."

She faced me completely, wrench hanging loosely at her side. "Then again, you also wouldn't start if I yanked out vital components and didn't replace them."

Did she just threaten me? "I'll leave you alone." I turned away.

"Are you fucking my mom?" Paige's question hit my back as hard as I imagined that wrench might.

I really didn't want to get into this with her. "That's between her and me." I faced her again.

"So, yes. Because otherwise you'd say *no*."

I made a point of clamping my mouth shut. Something told me there wouldn't be any winners in this conversation.

"Are you fucking Deacon?" Paige asked.

I was being interrogated by a seventeen year old. "Not currently." Though the question sent a spike of regret through me. "I'm talking to you." And wondering what the best way was to walk away without being rude.

Paige turned back to her bike, but her arms still hung at her sides. Were we done?

I opened my mouth to wish her a better day, so I could leave.

"What do you do when people don't act the way you expect them to?" She asked.

That was the million-dollar question, wasn't it? "I wish I knew."

Paige sank onto a nearby metal stool. "Did Mom tell you what happened at the dance?"

"No. You asked her not to." I was not equipped to handle teenage angst. I barely knew how to handle my own.

"So you do know how to give a straight answer."

"Nothing I do is completely straight. It's always at least a little bi." If I was making bad jokes, I was nervous.

The corners of Paige's mouth tugged up in an almost-smile.

"You don't have to laugh. No one actually likes that joke," I said.

This time she did smile. "You do, or you wouldn't use it more than once."

"I pun when I don't know what to say. Or make movie references." I pulled up a second stool and sat across from her.

She nodded at her motorcycle. "I leave. The bike takes me away from awkward conversation, except when it doesn't work."

I'd rarely related to something more. "Do you want to talk about it? I can make motorcycle noises if it helps."

Paige laughed. "You're just some random dude. Why would I talk to you?"

"I don't have a stake in the outcome."

"You're fucking my mom."

If she thought she could beat me at the talking in circles game, she was about to meet a master. "I thought I was just some random dude. Besides, I didn't say that, you did."

"You confirmed by denial. Why do you care what's pissing me off?" Paige said.

"I don't like to see people upset. And I promise if you choose to unload on me, I'm not going to judge or share your secrets. Not even with Brooke."

"Unless it's illegal or dangerous?"

I smirked. "Exactly."

Paige sighed. "Bryan likes this girl Jamie. And she's my best friend."

"Okay." Did she not want her brother dating her friends? That didn't line up with what Brooke started to say inside.

Paige twisted her mouth and her fingers. Silence stretched between us, and I tempered my patience.

"But apparently Jamie likes me and she kissed me and now Bryan hates me and I can't look Jamie in the eye and everyone else at school is stupid and I just want out of this dumb town." When Paige finally spoke the words tumbled out in a rush.

"I hated high school too."

Paige pursued her lips. "Hardly my point."

"I know." I was trying to fumble my way through

a conversation and not piss her off again. I really did feel where she was coming from, but I doubted she'd believe me if I just said so.

"You don't even get it." Paige's huff was full of frustration.

Then again, being direct was easier than trying to guess how to be sneaky. "I do. I've been there."

"You really hated high school? You're so smart."

"So are you. Do you not like Jamie?"

"She's my best friend," Paige said. "I like her enough to say that, and I swear to God if you ask me if I *like* like her…"

I wouldn't now. "Are you attracted to her?"

"I like boys. I had a boyfriend. I *really* liked kissing him."

I liked kissing boys too. And girls. This *really* wasn't a conversation I should be having with her. She needed someone closer to her. Not *some random dude*. "Okay."

"But I really liked kissing Jamie," Paige said.

"You're allowed to like both."

Paige growled. "I know that. But I don't like both."

I wanted to argue she just said exactly the opposite.

"Besides, Bryan likes her." Paige's voice grew quiet and all of the fight seemed to drain from her, leaving her looking deflated.

"This isn't about him." My conversations with Brooke and Deacon echoed in my mind. I was giving her advice I'd practiced, but I was also doubting my decision to push Deacon away the way I had. "So go find her and kiss her back and see what happens."

"But what about—"

"It doesn't matter," I said.

Paige scowled. "You don't know what I was going to say."

No, but I had a pretty good idea it was a protest having to do with her brother's feelings. "It doesn't matter," I repeated. "If you like the kiss, you can keep doing it. If you don't, you owe it to her to let her know. If Bryan doesn't like it, he needs to learn to deal because life isn't always what we want it to be. And if the uptight fucks at your school don't like it, fuck 'em. You're graduating in four months, make a memory or two that *you* want before then."

"Harsh."

Not really. "Honest."

"A lot of people don't like that kind of honesty," Paige said.

"Nope. Promise me you won't beat up the motor-cycle anymore?"

Paige's smile was back, and some of her tension was gone. "I promise. Thank you."

Now if only it were so easy to figure out my own confusion and take my own advice. I should forget about Deacon as anything more than a friend, and focus on Brooke.

But my mind rebelled at the thought.

23

deacon

WITH MOST OF the work done in the basement that required a crew, the next week was spent making sure the space was usable as an expansion to the showroom. The only big job left was reinforcing the stairs. Tuesday night, Evie helped Adam and I get those in place.

The rest of the week, he and I spent evenings fixing the place up. It was fun. A lot more fun than work should be, but that was one reason I enjoyed my shop—it wasn't a slog. But during the day when Adam went to visit Brooke, there was a smoldering ember inside me that burned for me to yank him back. To growl *mine*.

Except I didn't know if it was Adam or Brooke it wanted to yank away, and I wanted this feeling gone. It wouldn't serve anyone.

When he came back Friday night, he told me Brooke was cleared to walk around again, as long as she took it easy, and that she wanted to come see the work we'd done. That possessive spark roared to a flame with the reminder that a month ago, Brooke would have told me that directly and never given a second thought to if Adam knew. I smothered the feeling.

Saturday, mid-afternoon after most of the DIY-ers had finished their shopping, Adam headed to Evie's. His videos of Sebastian's had done so well that he was working his way through other shops on the street.

He'd wanted to do Aubrey's place next, and tie it into mine, but she wasn't answering texts or calls, and she managed to make herself busy anytime one of us stopped by.

I was trying to give her space to cool down, but I didn't want to be waiting. I wanted to make things right with her. I wanted Brooke back. I didn't want Adam going to visit...

Was I asking too much?

Absolutely. I needed to get my shit together.

Adam called a little before eleven.

"Yeah," I answered.

"Hey. Dylan is there, right?"

"Yes."

"This is running long," Adam said. "Will you go pick up Brooke?"

She can drive herself, can't she? I loathed the thought and that I'd had it the moment it entered my mind. Besides, I was more desperate to see her again than I wanted to admit. Which, of course I was. I missed a friend. "Yeah. No problem."

For some reason, *Brooke's just a friend, the same way Adam is* repeated in my head the entire drive to her house.

When I arrived, there was a car in her driveway I didn't recognize. A battered old sedan that looked like it had as much rust as mileage.

Brooke was talking to a man who was trying to shove a welded hunk of something into his back seat. Her smile was bright and he had her full attention.

He straightened up enough for me to get a good look. The guy was a solid wall of muscle, with cropped short hair. The hints of silver meant he was probably close to Brooke's age, and he could probably break her with those fucking upper arms.

A strange noise drew my attention and I realized I was growling. I swallowed the response, and climbed from my truck. Approaching with confidence, I continued to size him up until I reached him and Brooke.

"Deacon, *hey*." Her voice was bright and her smile had grown. "This is Quentin."

He extended his hand. "Pleasure. Where did you serve?"

I squeezed tightly to let him know I wouldn't be intimidated, and tried to make sense of his question. "Denny's, for about two weeks in high school? Waiting tables wasn't for me."

"Ah. I assumed…" He scrubbed a hand over his head.

Oh. Right. I forgot some days I had the military-style haircut. "No. I was never military." Was I picking on some old vet? "Much respect, though." I added quickly, making sure he knew I was sincere.

Brooke moved to stand next to me, facing Quentin. "Deacon did a charity stream with a friend for Christmas, and had to shave his head as part of it. A Konsoles for Kids thing."

I wanted to smirk in self-satisfaction. *See, I can help too.* But a charity stream was hardly equivalent to military duty, and why did I care what this Quentin guy thought or what Brooke thought of me compared to him?

"Cool." Quentin nodded.

"Thanks." My reply came out tight and didn't make any sense as a response to what he'd said. Apparently I was using up my good will.

Quentin gave the slightest shake of his head. "Anyway, I need to go. Great to meet you Deacon, and I'll see you around, Brooke."

"Remember, you're welcome any time." Brooke pulled Quentin into a tight hug that seared my insides with something muddy and heated. Especially when Quentin met my gaze over her shoulder, and raised an eyebrow.

My thoughts were still seething when he left, so I didn't realize Brooke was talking to me until she waved her hand in front of my face.

"Earth to Deacon," she called.

I yanked myself back together. "Right. What? Did you want to go, or do you need to… something?"

"I'm ready." Her tone sounded off.

Then again, mine probably did too. We climbed into my truck and the engine sputtered a few times before roaring to life. I pointed us toward my shop.

"Does Adam know about Quentin?" The question slipped past my lips without permission. I was barely okay with Adam and Brooke as a couple. Add another guy to the mix, one who could probably coax Brooke into all sorts of pretzely shapes—

Brooke gave a short, throat-clearing cough. "Does Adam know that I have friends? Presumably." Her voice was tight.

"I just mean…"

"What?" She asked. "What do you mean? Does Adam know I have friends with penises? He asked you to make sure I had a ride, so it seems that way. Adam doesn't dictate who I spend time with, and does it matter what my friends have hanging between their legs?"

Brooke had been gone for two weeks. I'd been pretending that entire time that I didn't need to go visit her, and now that she was sitting in my truck I was picking a fight. I forced myself to chill the fuck out. "It doesn't."

"Good." She tucked her hands into her lap.

"Exactly." I drove.

Brooke sighed.

And now there was that heavy, unnatural silence that I hated.

"How are things looking in your basement?" Brooke's tone was neutral.

I didn't want to fake a conversation for the sake of filling empty air. "Adam's probably already told you."

"I'm asking you. I want to hear if *you're* happy with the way things look and what *your* thoughts on the matter are."

I gripped the steering wheel until my knuckles ached, hoping I could get a grip on myself as well. "Things are going well." There, was that so hard? "I'm really happy with the way it all came together. The lighting looks great. Thank you for the wiring."

"Of course. Any time. Did you get any pushback from Travis?"

How much did she know? It didn't matter, because she asked for my thoughts. "He's doing his damndest to make everyone's lives miserable right now. I don't know if he's suffering from tiny dick syndrome or what."

"Really. You don't know that?" Brooke's tone was flat, but a hint of amusement undercut the words.

I shot her a puzzled look. "What? Why?"

"I'd just assume that at the very least he thinks he is. Or he's upset he didn't get an invite to the cool kids' party."

My laugh was half-entertained, half-disbelief. "I can promise you we're not the cool kids."

"From the outside, the people who own the shops on Main are very much the cool kids. Tattooed. Confident. High tech meets classy shops. You know you're all in enviable positions, right? You, Aubrey, Sebastian, Evie… All of you."

I'd never thought of it that way before. We were all struggling to stay open, especially with Travis and the council forcing new regulations, and our customers tended to be there as much for the novelty as the actual merchandise.

But I did love what I did, and most of them felt the same.

Not that it mattered. Regardless of how we saw ourselves, Travis's decrees wouldn't change. And really, as long as Brooke was smiling and joking with me again, I could think about everything else later.

When we got back to the antique shop, Adam had returned. He was behind the counter talking to Dylan when we walked in.

"You're back." The shift in Adan's expression when he saw Brooke, from casual to bright as sunshine, was unmistakable. He hopped from the stool he was sitting on, crossed the distance between us, and reached for her.

Brooke took a step away, and the frown that whispered across her face was mirrored in Adam's expression.

Was that because of me? There was no way they'd acted like this when Adam went to visit her. "You don't have to act any differently around me than you would if you were alone," I said. "If you're dating, you're dating."

Adan loosely grasped her fingertips.

Pursing her lips, Brooke looked past me, to Dylan. She moved further into the shop. "I don't know how public we're making things yet." Her voice was so soft I had to strain to make out the words.

I still wasn't sure I'd heard them right.

But based on the scowl etched on Adam's face, Brooke said exactly what I thought she did.

How dare she?

And why was as much of me cheering as upset? The surge of ambivalence was enough for me to choke on.

24

brooke

I WANTED to take my reactions to Adam back, but I couldn't, no matter how much hurt was in his gaze. What was I doing? Giving up someone amazing because...

Because of nothing. I closed the distance between us and brushed my lips over Adam's, relishing the spark that hadn't diminished at all in the last week.

He slipped his hand to the back of my neck, holding me in place, and deepened the kiss until the only thing, the only person who existed was him.

"You had me worried for a minute." His teasing was undercut with a more serious tone when he broke the kiss and moved his hands to mine.

"I'm gonna take a break," Dylan said nervously.

And that was at the root of my hesitation. Most of it. I forced a smile. "It's not that I'm not enjoying this, but people talk, and the twins and..."

And Deacon was watching us and I didn't dare

look at his reaction, after the way he reacted to Quentin.

"Deacon isn't people," Adam teased.

Deacon cleared his throat loudly. "Thanks."

"Not what I mean." Adam turned to him. "I mean you're not a fucking town gossip who's going to spread this everywhere, and Dylan's not either. You're not a generic being, you're Deacon."

I should better explain my reaction, but I wasn't sure I understood it myself. With Deacon next to me and Adam reaching for me, my brain stopped working when everything I wanted collided with everything I wasn't supposed to have.

It wasn't just about people talking, though I did worry about how gossip would come back on the twins, but it was about Deacon, which made me a freaking hypocrite. I adored what I had with Adam and wanted more.

"It's been a long time since I've dated—as we've discussed—and I'm feeling my way around how it works." That sounded reasonable, didn't it? It was the truth, so it had better.

And the way Adam wove his fingers with mine and squeezed my hand was both reassuring and warmed me with promises of more later. "It's perfectly reasonable," he said.

Deacon nodded. "I get it. Not that I need to, but I do."

Good. *Great* even. And maybe next time I was alone with Adam, we'd make it all the way to third base. A whisper in the back of my mind reminded me that probably meant giving up *lessons* with Deacon. That I was most likely already at that point. And the thought of that…

When did I turn into a sex fiend? Was this what a fifteen-plus year dry spell did to a woman?

Both Adam and Deacon were watching me. Crap, one of them had asked me something. "I'm sorry, what?" Did I need more sex or less to make sure I could pay better attention next time?

"Do you want the basement grand tour?" Deacon asked.

Are you hitting on me? The teasing question didn't make any sense, and even if it did, I had no idea how it would land. A few weeks ago, that kind of joke would've been normal, but now… "I'd like that, yes." I hid a wince at the formal language.

Neither of them looked fazed and I probably needed to stop thinking so much.

We headed toward the basement, and I could tell from that first step that things were different. For instance, I wasn't afraid I was going to fall through a stair on the way down. When we reached the bottom, Deacon flicked one of the switches I'd installed, and light flooded the entire room.

They led me through the new maze. There were a few walls in place, and the supports had been reinforced and made pretty, but mostly they'd left the entire place open, similar to upstairs. There was a lot more order to the furniture now, though. It was obvious that certain styles were grouped together and there was a flow to the room.

"I love it," I found myself saying over and over again. And when we reached the end of the tour, I asked, "When are you opening it to the public?"

"Unofficially on Monday, and we're making a bigger deal about it next weekend," Deacon said. "Adam's going to do a big series of videos."

It was perfect. I had so many questions. "Did you ever figure out how it all got down here in the first place? Do you know why no one told you there was a basement? Are you keeping any pieces for yourself?"

"No, no, and no." Deacon gave a faint smile.

This entire exchange felt stilted. I wanted him to make a joke. To flirt with me in a way I didn't know how to deal with. For Adam to pull an obscure movie reference out that I loved understanding. What were the odds the three of us could go back to the way things were without me giving up the new things as well? "I think I need another lesson."

White-hot embarrassment spread through me when I realized what I'd just said. Deacon and Adam looked shocked. I needed to back the heck up. "Not like that." Exactly like that. How horrible was I being? "I meant to go back to normal. Before…" I didn't want to dig this hole I was in deeper. "That was the original point, right? Teach me how to date without…" I sighed. "Without making an idiot of myself and alienating you." I looked at Deacon.

Adam brushed his lips over my cheek. "You're not being an idiot. This is weird for everyone."

"Speak for yourselves." Deacon deflated. "Yeah, okay. It's gotten weird, hasn't it? I have a solution, though."

Not that long ago, I would've expected a statement like that to lead to innuendo, that I wouldn't have known how to handle. I would've blushed, he would've winked, and the conversation would've moved on. "What are you thinking?"

"That." Deacon pointed to a couch. "That." He pointed to a wood and silk tri-fold screen.

Adam grinned. "Dim the lights, grab the projector."

The pieces clicked. "Movie night." Not something I'd ever done with them before. Nothing like back to the way things had been, but it felt right. I needed *right*. "I'm in. What are we watching?"

"*Samurai Cop*," Adam said without hesitation.

Deacon high-fived him. "*Yes.*"

"There's no way that's a real thing." No. Way. They'd thrown words together trying to be funny.

Adam's grin grew. "Oh, Brooke. Sweet, sweet, Brooke. Your world is about to be rocked."

"Or, it may feel more like rock-bottom, depending on how you feel about the movie." Deacon's tone was playful.

I was beyond intrigued. "Let's see this marvelous wonder you call *Ninja Cop*."

"*Samurai Cop*," Adam corrected me. "Very important detail. I'll grab my gear." He turned toward the stairs.

"I'll close the shop and call for food," Deacon said.

Adam gave me a quick kiss on the lips. "Don't go anywhere."

I perched on the edge of the couch while I waited. They weren't gone long. Within fifteen minutes, Deacon had an assortment of wings, Adam had his laptop hooked up to a small HD projector, and they had arranged the furniture so we could watch.

The guys sat on either side of me, and Adam started the movie.

"There'll be lines through the movie." I nodded at the tri-fold divider with opening credits reflected off it.

"It doesn't even matter. I promise you." Adam handed me a plate piled with food.

That seemed unlikely, but they seemed to know what they were doing.

For the next hour and half, I watched in amazement and horror, mixed with the frequent laugh of disbelief, at the mess that played out in front of us.

When it was over, I stared at the silk screen where images had been seconds earlier, and blinked rapidly in disbelief. "What did we just watch?"

"Epic, right?" Adam asked.

Deacon snorted. "So bad it's good."

"Softcore porn?" I was still processing. "Meets eighties sitcom? With bad editing?"

"More or less." Adam didn't sound bothered at all. "You laughed."

"Because it was *bad*."

"That's the point," Deacon said. "Hilariously bad."

It was starting to make sense. A little. *Samurai Cop* kept playing in my mind, as much as I wanted to forget it. "And then he brought out a cake, and sang *Happy Birthday*, wearing nothing but a thong."

"You mean that didn't turn you on, baby?" Deacon's tone was instantly over-the-top seductive in a not-quite Austin Powers kind of way.

I made a fake gagging noise. "I know you're not even a little serious right now."

Adam tugged me into his lap, as if it were the most natural thing. Then again, it had become that. He trailed his nose lightly up my neck. "You don't want some sexy hunk of beef in practically nothing bringing you cake in bed?"

"I mean…" How was I supposed to answer that? It felt like a trick question.

"I do." Adam nipped my earlobe.

He was saying one thing, but was it what he meant to say?

"Wait. Do you want to be the sexy hunk, or be served by the sexy hunk?" Deacon voiced the question in my head.

Adam puffed out his cheeks and exhaled slowly, his brow furrowed. "That's a tough call. On the one hand, you look really good in practically nothing, and on the other, I'm not sure I trust you to bake a cake."

"Fuck you." Deacon laughed. "I'd bake an amazing cake."

What did I just hear? My brain backed up. It was exactly what I'd been missing—the flirting banter without hesitation—and on the one hand I liked the potential behind it and on the other hand I wondered why I thought it was okay. "Did you just hit on someone else while I was sitting in your lap?"

"Yes?" Adam seemed unfazed. "Don't get me wrong, I'd happily eat your cake—take that as you will--and even more happily watch you walk around in practically nothing." He slid a hand lightly up my inner thigh. "But you won't fill out a banana hammock the same way Deacon will." He teased his fingers lightly over my crotch.

Oh, jeez. I gasped at his playful touch. "Banana hammock? Seriously?" I tried to force the laughter into my voice, but I was falling into fantasies of both of them undressed, enhanced by every caress Adam laid through my clothing.

"Whale tail?" Deacon asked.

"Butt floss?" Adam added.

I laughed. "This is the education I never knew I needed. Slang terms for *thong*."

"You're welcome." Deacon gave me a seated bow.

Adam danced his fingertips down my spine. "Or did you have something else in mind when you asked for another lesson?"

Yes. This felt like a trap. Asking for what I wanted was a fast track to losing an incredible opportunity with Adam before we could even explore what we had. But he was the one who brought us back to this point in the conversation.

What was the right answer?

25
adam

MORE SEX SEEMED like the next logical step in this relationship.

Sex with both Brooke and Deacon.

Then again, my dick was rock hard from the way she pressed against me and I couldn't stop thinking about how incredible the last couple of times had been, so it was possible *logical* actually meant *the only thing I could think about with all the blood rushing to my cock*.

Possible.

But that didn't mean I was wrong.

Besides, it was obvious that the two of them were still attracted to each other, regardless of what they told themselves or me. There was no way in Hell I was letting someone as amazing as Brooke go, but I was starting to think I felt more than friendship for Deacon, and not just because the sex was good.

So, yeah, I was going to push for more from both

of them. More time spent together, more movies, more fucking, more of Deacon dominating her and bowing to me, more Brooke squirming in pain and screaming in pleasure.

Just *more*.

But Brooke hadn't answered my question and Deacon was unusually quiet, so I was going to nudge a little harder.

"We should head upstairs," I said. When Deacon frowned and opened his mouth, I realized I needed to say more. "All three of us."

Brooke didn't move. "What's upstairs?"

"A lot more room to maneuver and furniture that we can get stains on without ruining Deacon's livelihood." I liked clever euphemisms and flirting, but at some point, things had to be said plainly.

"Why would we get stains— *Oh*." Brooke ducked her head, but it didn't hide her blush.

She was wonderful. The perfect combination of bold and strong meets sweet and innocent

I looked at Deacon. "You and I did promise to show Brooke what the candles were for besides light when the power went out."

He furrowed his brow and bit his bottom lip.

"It can't be that hard a decision." I was surprised by his hesitation.

"It's not. Or rather, *something's* hard, but…"

Brooke pushed away from me and stood. I wasn't sure if I should be excited or disappointed.

"Are we allowed to do this?" she asked.

Disappointed. Or confused. "Why wouldn't we be?"

She shrugged. "I thought you and I were..." She sighed. "A couple."

"I did too." I needed to remember I couldn't make assumptions about people seeing the world the way I did. "I'm pretty sure that means we are. But if I want to have sex with both you and Deacon, and you want to have sex with Deacon and me, and Deacon wants... You see where this is going... If all three of us agree, it seems like we're allowed to do it."

"Then why don't more people do it?" Brooke asked. "It's obviously really incredible."

"Because more people don't agree." About a lot of things, but this wasn't the time to get philosophical. I stood and grasped her hands. "But if you're not interest—"

"I am. I very much am."

Deacon let out a short laugh.

I shot him a look that I hoped conveyed *don't you dare make her feel bad or dumb about this.*

He looked back with wide eyes that I hoped just as much meant *I wouldn't ever.* "A little rope and a lot of wax sounds like a perfect next step to the evening, in my opinion."

"Rope?" Brooke's voice came out in a squeak and the pink of her flush spread along her neck and arms.

This was going to be so much fun.

I grasped one of her hands and Deacon took the other, and we led her upstairs. With each step, my cock rubbed against my zipper with agonizing friction. After a week of make-out sessions, I was ready to explode from anticipation.

Especially if Deacon was involved.

In my bedroom, I pulled out the trunk with my supplies, and set the wax up to start melting. Next I grabbed a worn, comfortable blanket from the same box. The comforter wasn't anything special—it came from a thrift store—but I used it exclusively for play, so laying it on the bed made me harder.

I tossed a bundle of silk rope on top of it, and turned to Brooke. "This is the same as before—if you want to stop, you tell me. You have to tell me or I won't know." It sounded obvious, but the rules were important to drive home.

She was flushed and her lips glistened from where she kept running her tongue over them. "Okay."

I knelt at her feet and undid the laces on her boots. I helped her step out one shoe at a time, followed by her socks, and Deacon tugged her shirt over her head. Last, I pushed her jeans to the ground.

Brooke was wearing a matching pink bra and panty set, trimmed with lace and just a few shades darker than her skin. I could be dim, but I recognized exactly what the underwear meant—she'd been prepared to tell me *yes* tonight.

I'd have to make sure not to disappoint.

"Fuck, you're gorgeous," Deacon muttered.

The fact that I was hard enough to drill a hole

through the floor with my cock reinforced how much I agreed.

Brooke clasped her hands in front of her, managing demure in practically nothing.

Fuck, this woman…

"Lingerie stays on," I said. "Protect the more sensitive bits." Though I couldn't help but glide a hand under the elastic of her waistband, along her bare skin, making her shiver.

"On your back. Middle of the bed," I ordered.

Brooke complied.

Deacon tied her hands together and secured them above her head.

I glided my palms down her thighs, along her calves, and to her ankles, kissing along the same path I touched, before securing her feet wide apart to the bed frame. "Deacon's right."

"About a lot of things," Brooke said. "What specifically?" There was a quiver in her voice.

I studied her, bound and at our mercy. "You are gorgeous and I'm already thinking of tying you up like this again and again, and all the things we can do to you." I meant to say *I* could do to her, but I didn't want to correct myself.

"Me too," Deacon said. "Except yours probably hurt a little more."

I raised an eyebrow. "How do you figure?"

"Only one of us is a sadist."

I shrugged. "Your loss. Besides, you like watching."

Deacon grinned. "Guilty."

"You're in luck, because it's showtime." I grabbed a bottle of baby oil, poured a generous amount in my hand, and handed the bottle to Deacon.

"Is that part of the play?" Brooke asked.

"Yes." I worked my way up one of her legs while Deacon started on her stomach. "And it's part of the clean-up."

He and I took our time covering her generously with oil and making her moan and glisten in the process.

I grabbed one of the candles, and the wax that had pooled at the base. "I love painting a blank canvas, but I've never had one that looks like you before," I said to Brooke.

"Painting?"

"With all the pretty colors." I dribbled a few light drops along her arms, where she should be less sensitive, to gauge her response.

She sucked in a sharp breath through her teeth when the hot wax hit her skin. *Fuck* I loved that sound and the way she instinctively jerked against the ropes. It was incredible, hearing her and watching her stretched out for me to do with as I pleased.

I moved to her ribs next, alternating between rhythmic drips of color, and drizzled lines. Then down to her stomach. Each time wax hit her skin, Brook squirmed and whimpered.

"Does it hurt?" I asked.

Her *yes* was a jolt of want inside. "But not in a bad way," she said.

She might as well have taken my entire length in her mouth.

The longer I worked, the more I fell into it. I didn't want to talk, I wanted to paint. To pick out those spots on Brooke that were soft, tender, and extra sensitive. Along her pelvis. The tops of her breasts. Her inner thighs.

The sounds she made were incredible, and the design that lay in front of me was more stunning than anything that hung in The Louvre.

She was writhing and panting and tugging against the ropes.

Fuck I needed her.

I barely had enough sense to roll on a condom after I freed my cock. Note to self—next time ask beforehand if we could do this without protection. With a tug in the right place, the ropes on her legs fell away. I shoved her panties aside, and thrust my cock inside her.

She was so slick and tight, and felt *so* good. I wanted to hammer until I was spent, but instead I rested there, and moved my thumb to her clit. I teased and coaxed and stroked, watching her in fascination as her breathing grew more shallow. As the colors flexed and moved and broke along her skin. As she clenched her hands into tight fists and tugged against the ropes.

And when she came, her scream of pleasure was

as delicious as her grunts of pain had been. She clenched around me, and I pushed her harder, drawing out her orgasm until she tried to pull away. I coaxed her into another orgasm, and when I felt her squeeze me for a second time, in a powerful clench, I pressed her knees to her chest and fucked her hard.

I let go of the last of my restraints and lost myself in her. In knowing Deacon watched us while he stroked himself. He hadn't come yet—he knew better.

Need tightened in my muscles and in my balls, coiling through me until I was wound tight and ready to snap. Orgasm tore from me, and I slammed inside Brooke with abandon, until I was spent.

I paused for a moment to catch my breath, then leaned in and pressed my lips to the hollow of her neck, behind her ear. "I think Deacon wants you too."

Her laugh was faint and light. "Okay." Her voice was soft.

I moved aside. Watching Deacon take my place and penetrate Brooke was incredible, especially knowing what he was feeling as she wrapped around him.

I reached above her head and untied her wrists, and she immediately moved her hands to clench the comforter in tight fights. Watching her take another man—no, Deacon specifically—knowing that he'd waited for this chance, was almost enough to make me hard again, despite my being spent.

Especially with the colors still splashed across her skin, some broken and some still intact.

And when Deacon came, hard and loud, pushing Brooke into climax again, it was an incredible sight.

He rolled over next to her, and we all lay there for a moment, the hum of the boiler keeping our heavy breathing company.

I forced myself to move. This next bit was as important as anything else—me coming down and making sure Brooke could do the same. Deacon and I were gentle about peeling the wax away, wiping Brooke clean, and rubbing aloe on any red marks that lingered.

As we pulled off her bra and panties, we couldn't help another round of play. Deacon sucked on her nipples and teased her breasts while I fingered her to orgasm again. She didn't say anything, but she made some delicious sounds. She was lost in the pleasure.

I needed to tug her back, but gently, so I lay behind her and pulled her into me. Deacon and I made soft, meaningless conversation, and eventually Brooke joined in.

I'd done things like this more than a few times in my life, both with and without the sex. But with Brooke, with Deacon, it was different. I didn't want something with just one of them—I wanted them both. On an ongoing basis.

The thought gripped me hard and refused to let go.

Curling up with Brooke and Deacon was definitely one of my favorite things. "We should make a habit of this." I was playing a teensy bit dirty, testing the waters while everyone was still glowing from sex. Or it was a strategic choice. Yeah, I liked that better, especially since I was already addicted to having both of them in my bed.

Brooke leaned more weight into me. "I wouldn't mind." Her voice was soft. Almost dream-like.

She'd probably agree to a lot in this state of mind, so I needed to be careful and make sure we hashed out details when she was thinking more clearly. But her words warmed me regardless.

Until I looked at Deacon. His expression was neutral at best and honestly it was more like a scowl hiding behind a mask. "You two should enjoy that." His tone was cool.

Brooke stiffened in my arms.

I didn't blame her for the reaction. "Pretty sure you're here with us." I kept my tone light. "You're going to tell me you hated every minute that led up to that orgasm?" I poured the teasing into my voice, but I also used severe language on purpose.

"Nope. The orgasms were amazing," Deacon said quickly. "Mine. Everyone's." Despite the lift to his reply, there was still an edge.

I didn't want to argue. I wanted to enjoy the bliss that came from what we'd just done. It was time to let this slide and go back to cuddling.

"But at some point between tonight and tomorrow morning"—Deacon had other ideas apparently—"I go back to my bed and the two of you do whatever it is you're doing."

"Right now we're lying here with you," I said.

"But he's got a point." Brooke no longer sounded like she was wrapped in happy clouds.

Deacon smirked, but his eyes were cold. "See?"

I wasn't sure I did. "See what?"

"It's okay." Brooke seemed to have absorbed Deacon's mood. "I knew what I was doing with Deacon. Learning how to navigate the dating world."

"Exactly." Deacon cut the word off. "We set those rules up front, and the two of you are fantastic together so mission accomplished."

"School's out," Brooke said.

I didn't like any of this. Was I the asshole here? No. I wasn't the one refusing to see what the three of us could have.

Deacon climbed from my bed. "Speaking of, I'll be in my room. You two crazy kids enjoy your night."

"Don't—"

I was cut off by him softly closing my bedroom door.

Brooke pressed into me again. "Final lesson learned," she muttered so quietly I didn't know if I was meant to hear it.

I pressed my lips to her forehead and tried not to drown in frustration.

26

deacon

IN THE MORNING, Adam's bedroom door was open, and he and Brooke were nowhere to be found.

Fine. Perfect. I got quiet time.

Then again, I'd had plenty of that last night, and all the way up until about five this morning when I finally drifted to sleep from exhaustion.

And none of the tossing and turning in bed had helped me figure out why I was so upset that I'd made the right decision, walking away after sex.

Their life wasn't mine. And Adam and Brooke really did look happy together.

What if I could be happy too?

I was happy, and the life in front of them wasn't my path to walk. It was dangerous to entertain dreams of a family, because it would hurt so badly when it didn't happen. Sure, what I was feeling now sucked and I couldn't define the feeling or why, but it was better than the pain I'd feel if I let myself believe I could have more.

It wasn't like I was going to wake up one morning and have the happy, traditional family I used to fantasize about.

It was best I stop sleeping with both Brooke and Adam now. Sure things would be tense for a little while, but then we could go back to the way things were. I didn't want to lose their friendship. That meant far more to me than getting laid sometimes.

And that went for both of them. I couldn't imagine Brooke would be okay with me having a friends-with-benefits relationship with her boyfriend.

I grabbed my coffee and headed down to the shop. While I was deciding where to start, since the shop was closed today, Adam came back. Time to be civil and friendly and start the path toward *we can still be friends*.

"Hey," I called cheerfully.

He didn't pause near the counter, heading toward the back instead. "Hey." He disappeared through the door that led upstairs.

Okay.

I got back to work.

A moment later Adam returned with his camera and laptop bags slung over his shoulder. "I'm heading to Aubrey's to film." He practically bounced rather than standing still.

Aubrey. Right. Someone else I'd fucked up my friendship with. "Tell her I said *hi*."

Adam gave me a look I didn't understand. "Or tell her yourself and make things right while you're there."

"I tried that already."

Adam sighed. "Yeah. All right. I'll be back."

"What was that?" I didn't know how to interpret his tone.

"A sigh."

Great. I was trying to be friendly and he was being defensive. "Why?"

"You don't want to know." Adam adjusted the straps on his shoulder, but didn't turn away.

I could let him go. That seemed like the logical thing to do. Wish him a genuine *have fun at Aubrey's* and let both of us get back to what we were doing. "I do want to know. It's why I asked."

"Do you keep pushing your friends away so you can ignore your commitment issues?"

I stared at him in disbelief. "What are you, my therapist?"

"Your friend."

I was starting to wonder. "Aubrey hit on me, and I was honest about how I felt. Is that my fault? Did you see that coming?"

"No."

"And she refuses to talk to me now. I tried to apologize."

Adam shrugged. "Try harder."

Frustration seared through me and I swallowed a growl. "What the fuck do you expect me to do?"

"Maybe admit that Br—ey, Aubrey's friendship is important, and do more than toss out a couple of obligatory words to make things right."

And of course this wasn't really about Aubrey. I clenched my jaw. "Just fucking go."

I clenched and unclenched my fist several times as Adam walked out the front door.

It didn't matter. There was work to do. The place needed to be straightened, so I could bring up a few show pieces from the basement. The delicate glass collectables in the front window needed to be dusted, I had to catch up on some inventory—

And why the fuck was this place so cluttered?

The thought caught me off-guard and my brain stumbled.

There was an order to the chaos, and it was mine. I'd never had an issue with it before. In a way, it reminded me of Adam—eclectic, diverse, and all over the place.

I clenched my fist harder, until my nails dug into my palm, and forced myself to take several deep breaths through my nose.

The *Addams Family* theme filled the shop, indicating someone had arrived, and I pasted on a pleasant smile.

Until Travis came into view.

"We're closed." I couldn't find a thread of pleasantness for him.

"With any luck, permanently soon."

This time I didn't try to fight my growl. "What can I do for you?"

His smile was too bright and friendly. "I'm working my way down the street this morning to remind everyone of the upcoming deadline for the next step in meeting the new building requirements. I notice no one has started yet. *No one.* And I find that disconcerting given the clause that requires you to sell if you can't comply with the rules."

"I'm sure everyone is working hard on next steps." I might be in a pissy mood, but that didn't mean I'd sell out my neighbors.

"Are you sure? Because I hear rumors of a basement remodel, and it seems like that time would've been better spent on bringing your shops up to the new code."

"Have you ever run an antique shop before, Travis?"

He scoffed. "No."

"A hardware store? A tea shop? A clothing boutique?"

Travis raised his brows. "Your point is?"

"I don't tell you how to be an asshole, you don't get to dictate how we upgrade our buildings."

"But I do. That's literally part of my job. I don't know why these people look up to you, but I know they're more likely to listen to you than me. I'll continue my way down the street, but reinforce with your friends that I'm fine with shutting you all down if you can't comply with the city's building codes, both structurally and visually," Travis said.

I gave him a tight-lipped grin and did some quick math in my head. Was the pay-off of using him as a punching bag, to work out my frustration, worth the cost of the consequences?

Probably not, but if he stuck around I'd want to find out anyway. "I have work to do. You know where the door is."

Travis snorted. "I'm fine with things if you keep ignoring this. I win either way."

I didn't give him the satisfaction of looking back at him, and a moment later, I heard his footsteps retreat and the door chime sounded again.

As much as I hated the words, Travis was right. The only reason I knew I had a basement was because Brooke helped me go looking for a way to pay for a remodel, and two weeks later, I was barely closer to getting there. I needed to crack the books and figure out next steps.

At least it would distract me from the nagging in the back of my brain that insisted on replaying last night and the conversation with Adam over and over for no reason other than to torture me.

My cellphone rang, and I hesitated when I saw Brooke's name on the screen.

Fuck it. "Hey." I kept my tone neutral.

"Deacon. I need your help."

My gut sank at the panic in her voice.

27

brooke

WHEN I STEPPED in my house, Paige and Jamie were asleep in the living room. Not unusually—Jamie had been sleeping over since the girls were little—but the two of them sleeping together on the couch was new.

I should be upset at the sight, right? It was adorable. My only real concern was how Bryan had reacted. It seemed strange that Paige would flaunt any part of this relationship after his reaction.

When I closed the door behind me and locked it, Paige sat up with a start. She looked around the room, her wide-eyed gaze finally falling on me. She looked panicked.

"It's okay. Just me," I said softly.

Jamie was stirring too.

"Oh my God, I'm so glad you're home. I was worried." Paige sounded more worried than she looked, and that was a high bar.

I gave her a reassuring smile. "Pretty sure that's

my line." I'd sent her a text last night and she responded, so she knew I'd be gone for the night.

Jamie sat up and squeezed Paige's hand.

Okay, that was adorable. My baby girl had a girlfriend. Given how worried she looked, now probably wasn't the time to coo over them and try to take pictures.

"Bryan saw your message, and"—Paige glanced at Jamie—"He was really mad last night. He left and he never came back."

Things had quieted down between the twins over the last week. The shouting had stopped, though they weren't quite on speaking terms yet, and I'd thought they were getting back to normal.

I didn't like the sound of *never came back.* "He didn't tell you where he was going?" How did I miss that their car wasn't in the driveway? Because I just expected it to be there or because I'd been too wrapped up in Adam to pay attention to important things.

"He said he was going to Lucas's house, but when he left he was so mad, I was worried," Paige said. "Especially when he wouldn't answer my texts."

This wasn't a big deal. "I'll call and make sure he's okay." I wanted to ask Paige if this was what it looked like with her and Jamie; it wouldn't do to make assumptions.

Paige glanced next to her and then down at where her hand was tangled with Jamie's. Paige's eyes grew wide again. "I can explain this." She held up their hands.

"Only when you're ready." I wasn't worried about Paige dating Jamie as long as they were happy, but I was worried about Bryan. "Go get dressed, I'll call your brother, and make breakfast."

"Thank you, Ms. Mansell." Jamie gave me a quick wave and the girls hurried upstairs.

I was definitely taking pictures later. I called Bryan's phone and there was no answer. My worry slipped back—the twins were required to pick up when I called, unless they were driving or working. It seemed unlikely Bryan was still asleep, and he might be driving home, but not if he was mad enough to storm out last night.

I just needed to know he was all right. I called Lucas's mother.

"Morning," Kandace answered in a pleasant tone.

"Hey, it's Brooke. I just need to make sure Bryan's all right." There was no reason to mask my worry, she'd understand.

The silence that came back wasn't reassuring.

"I assume you think he's here," Kandace finally said. "Hang on, let me make sure." I heard her muffled shout of *Lucas*. There was some mumbling. "I haven't seen him in days, and Lucas says he's not around."

Crap. Okay, he must've given Paige the wrong friend's name because he was sulking. "Okay, thank you."

"Brooke." Kandace's tone stopped me before I could hang up. "Call me if you need h—anything."

"I'm sure he's fine. Thank you, though." This wasn't a big deal. I wasn't the mom who freaked out about little things. Bryan had a lot of friends, and I'd only called one.

Ten of his closest friends later with no answer, and no call back from Bryan, and I was willing to admit this wasn't a little thing and I was worried.

I set two plates of pancakes on the table in front of Paige and Jamie, and tried to think of what to try next.

"You could trace his phone." Jamie looked as at home here as she ever had.

And she was a brilliant young woman. I should've done that first. I pulled up the finder app on my phone and told it to look for Bryan.

It pinged with a response telling me the device was less than fifty feet away. What the hell? Would I like to make the device ring? Yes, I very much would.

A muffled chime came from somewhere in the house, and I followed the noise to his room. His phone was sitting on his dresser.

Shit.

This was okay. Bryan was my straight A, never did anything wrong, baby boy. He was fine and I was missing something obvious. I called Colin, who hadn't seen Bryan. None of my sisters had either. Or my parents.

Panic was setting in.

I called the police and explained the basics of the situation.

"He's a nearly eighteen-year-old boy with a car, and it's Sunday," the officer said kindly but less than helpfully. "He's fine. Call us again if he's still not back tomorrow morning."

"What? No. He could be dead by then." Yes, that was where my mind was going.

Gregory laughed. "He's not dead, Brooke. He's probably just blowing off steam because of the rumors."

"The… rumors?"

"You know. About you and the guys down on Main Street. You had to know."

I didn't listen to the town gossip, especially when my name was attached to it, but that wasn't good. Apparently Travis had told everyone what I said after all, about sleeping with both Adam and Deacon. "You people need something else to do besides talk about your neighbors. My son is missing."

"Call back tomorrow morning, and maybe stop acting like the town slut." The line went dead.

I'd be furious about his commentary later, when I knew where Bryan was. I needed someone to help who wasn't one of his friends possibly hiding him, but who knew most of the town and had a knack for getting answers out of anyone.

The town had been talking about me, and it had probably gotten back to the kids. The last thing I wanted. Shit, shit, shit.

I dialed Deacon, ignoring the twinge about how things ended between us last night. It didn't matter. When he answered, I said, "I need your help." It was impossible to keep the worry out of my voice.

"Of course." His answer came without hesitation. Without ever asking *with what*?

I almost cracked when I explained what was going on, because he was kind and concerned the entire time.

"Come down to the shop," he said. "Bring Paige. We'll get everyone together and search."

I appreciated the idea but, "I don't know that walking the streets calling his name is the most efficient use of our time."

"Good point. I'll talk to everyone I know, ask if they've seen him or his car, and then Adam and I are coming over."

"Thank you." When I hung up, I pressed my back to the wall and sank to the floor.

"Mom?"

I looked up to find Paige studying me with concern. "Hey. Did you girls eat?"

Paige shook her head. "Jamie went home."

And I didn't hear it? I was a shitty mom.

"Is Bryan all right?" Paige asked.

Lord, I hoped so. "I'm sure he is."

"You're lying. Do you want me to call hospitals?"

My insides twisted in on themselves at the thought, but it needed to be done. "No. I'll do that.

Help me think of anyone at school who might have any idea where he is."

"Okay." Paige wandered a few feet away, then paused. "He's fine. I'd know if he wasn't fine. Wouldn't I?"

I nodded. "I'm sure you would."

Paige didn't look any more convinced than me as she and I started making more calls.

When Adam and Deacon showed up, neither Paige nor I had any more answers. It should be a relief since it meant Bryan wasn't in a nearby hospital, but not knowing was eating me alive.

"Any luck?" Adam asked.

I shook my head.

"I thought you said he took the car," Deacon said.

Why would he say that? My brain stalled and I looked at Paige.

She shrugged. "He did."

"It's parked behind the barn. We saw the tail end of it when we pulled in." Deacon nodded in that direction.

No. I hadn't missed that. There was no way. But why would Deacon lie?

Paige's worried expression had morphed, and she was looking between me, Adam, and the door. "I'll go look in the barn," she said.

I couldn't imagine why Bryan would be in there. Had he parked the car out of sight and decided to camp in the woods behind the house, like when they were little? That didn't make sense, but it made more sense than him being in the barn. "The barn is off limits."

"I'll go with her, to make sure it's safe," Adam said.

Deacon frowned. "You didn't check everywhere on the property?"

I did *not* need his judgment right now. "Because that place is supposed to be boarded up. No one goes in there."

"I'm sure he didn't." Paige was lying. "But I'll just go make sure. Adam will help."

I was an idiot for not having looked myself. "I'll go." I was already heading toward the door, trying not to jump to conclusions and not sure what I hoped to find.

My son, of course, but why did it feel like it wouldn't be that simple?

Paige trailed behind me, as did the men. When I reached the barn doors, they pushed open without so much as a squeak. Light spilled in through the windows up top, casting the entire room in long shadows and falling on...

Bryan?

What the hell was he sitting on top of?

"Is that a tank in my barn?" Worry had made me hallucinate. That was the only explanation. When no one answered, I scrubbed my eyes and looked again. It looked real enough.

Hours of concern shattered any hold I had on

restraint. "Why is there a tank in here?" I asked again. "And where the fuck have you been, Bryan?"

He worked his jaw and pieces clicked in my head.

I whirled on Paige before Bryan could answer. "You knew this was here." I looked at Adam. "And so did you." I *knew* that was true. I turned back to Bryan, not giving anyone a chance to reply. Ebbing worry was becoming white-hot anger. "I've been calling hospitals." I could be furious now that I knew he was safe. "Why the fuck is there a tank in my barn?"

"Brooke." Deacon's calm voice was the last thing I expected—wanted—to hear.

I focused on him. "Thank you for your help, but I swear to God if you tell me to calm down…"

He held up his hands, as if in surrender. "I wouldn't dream of it."

"Good." I pointed to the twins. "Both of you, in the house *now*." I was torn between screaming and letting ice fill my voice. "Deacon will make sure you get there, because apparently no one else here can be trusted to do that. If I find either of you using your phones when you get in the house, this will be so much worse for you."

"Mom. I'm so—"

"*Now*." I cut Bryan off.

As the twins stalked from the barn with Deacon following, I gave Adam my full attention. "There's a fucking tank in my barn." I didn't care that I was repeating myself. Who had time to keep track of words when my world had just crumbled unnecessarily and been shoved back together again? "I thought my son was dead somewhere. I was going to call every hospital in the state. And he was asleep in a barn he's not supposed to go in, with a tank that you fucking knew about."

"Brooke." There was apology in his tone.

And I didn't want to hear it. Fury and relief were bleeding away the adrenaline rush I'd been riding for hours. "No." If I listened to him, if I looked at him for too long, I'd remember I cared about him, and there were so many reasons that was a bad idea. "I have to deal with my children."

Adam walked back to the house with me, and instinct wanted me to drift closer, but I was angry, tired, confused, and relieved, and that all made me a little ill.

Deacon was waiting for us in the living room, and the twins were nowhere to be found. He jerked a thumb toward the stairs. "In their rooms. I told them to leave their doors open so you could see them."

"Thank you." I found enough energy to sound sincere, but I couldn't keep the fury from my voice. "I've got it from here."

He stepped in my path, and I gritted my teeth. It seemed unlikely he could say anything to help right now.

"I know you don't want to hear it, but you need to stop, breathe, and cool down," Deacon said.

I gave him a dangerous, disbelieving grin. "You can go now."

Deacon didn't move. "Bryan did this for a reason. If you go up there right now, in this mood, will it help?"

Wow, I *could* be more angry. Surprise. "Who the fuck are you to tell me how to raise my children? *My* children. Not yours." A teensy part of me recognized I shouldn't take this out on him, and that he may even have a point—even if it wasn't his place to open his mouth—but it was easy to ignore all of that.

"Okay." Deacon moved. Smart man. "We're leaving unless you need anything else."

"I'm—"

I glared at Adam, silencing him. "Don't. Seriously. Just. Go," I said.

Adam reached for me and I stepped away.

Deacon grabbed his arm and tugged him toward the door.

With the house silent, and the twins safe, everything drained from me at once, and I sank onto the bottom step of the stairs. I wanted to scream and cry and rage and laugh. But I didn't have anything left.

I should go talk to Bryan. To Paige. Deacon was right about screaming being counterproductive. Instead of moving, I dropped my head into my hands.

The day rushed into my mind in a single, suffocating onslaught. The way the morning started waking up next to Adam. How cute it was finding Paige with someone she cared about. The growing horror of realizing Bryan was missing, the calls, the gossip, Adam lying to me…

I fisted clumps of my hair, tugging until my scalp ached.

The thoughts didn't stop.

I should've seen some of this—that Bryan wasn't happy, that Paige was changing, that the twins had managed to put a tank in my barn—but I was too busy spending my time screwing around. I wanted to learn how to date, and my kids had needed me.

What kind of horrible mother did that make me?

Footsteps sounded behind me, soft on the carpet like someone who'd learned where all the creaks in the floor were over the years.

Had Paige been sneaking out?

I couldn't deal with that possibility on top of everything else.

She sat next to me on the stairs. "I'm sorry," she said softly.

"For what?" As far as I could tell, she was the most innocent in all of this. "You didn't do anything."

"I made Bryan mad, by dating Jamie."

"No. Don't ever feel bad about that." At least I could do one thing right. "He doesn't get a say in who you date. Ever."

Paige laughed weakly. "But he wouldn't have left last night otherwise. Besides, the tank is my fault. The fact that Adam kept it a secret is my fault. I wasn't going to use it for anything bad; it was supposed to be a surprise. It's not loaded, the gun doesn't work as far as I know, but I wanted to restore it. I wanted to prove to everyone that I could. I made Adam promise—"

"You're also not responsible for him lying to me." There was a block in my head angry at me for falling for him, and needing it to be his fault.

Paige leaned into me. "I'm still sorry. I didn't want to upset you. Have you ever said *fuck* that much before?"

"Probably not in the entirety of my life." I wrapped an arm around her shoulder. "You should've told me you had a tank."

"Am I in trouble?"

"Yes."

"Grounded?"

I was tempted to ground both of them for the next several months, just so I'd always know where they were. "No. But you do have to go clean up the breakfast no one ate and do the dishes."

"Now?"

I kissed her on the forehead. "Now." My voice was soft.

Paige headed into the kitchen, and I pushed to my feet to go talk to Bryan. He was lying on his bed, staring at the ceiling.

"Why did you have to call *them*?" he asked.

"Because I thought you were dead in a ditch somewhere and I knew they could help."

Bryan rolled his head to the side and looked at me. "Every time that truck pulls into our driveway, the entire town talks about you."

"The entire town has been talking about me since I dared move here with two children and no husband."

"And yet, you keep doing the things that make them talk. And you let Paige do them."

"Enough." I would let him air his frustrations, but some statements couldn't go unchallenged. "Paige is hardly flaunting her relationship, and even if she is, she has as much of a right as anyone. And I've been friends with Deacon for a long time."

"But you've only been bragging about sleeping with him recently."

Ice settled in the pit of my stomach. I'd like to argue I hadn't bragged, but that was exactly what I'd done to Travis.

"And maybe you don't like it here, and if so, why did you drag us here? Because now I'm here, and I like it here, and unlike Paige I'm not desperate to leave, and I don't like having to hear people talk about you." Bryan's voice was raw.

There was a lot to unpack there. "I can't live my life based on what other people think." The words were easy to say, but today they dug deep, insisting I give them a closer look and be a little more honest with my son and myself. I didn't have the time for that.

"But every time someone calls you the town slut, I have to decide whether to pretend I don't care, or deck them. You're lucky the only thing I did was hide in the barn."

"Don't you dare threaten me." I didn't want to get

mad again. "We're having a civil conversation, and you can be an adult about it."

Bryan sat up and swung his legs over the edge of the bed. "I'm surprised you noticed. I'm surprised you noticed I was gone."

Guilt met reemerging anger. "Of course I noticed." Deacon's words echoed in my thoughts. Yelling wasn't going to make this better, but I so badly wanted to. "I was worried about you. We called most of the town, and every hospital in a fifty-mile radius, looking for you. That's why Deacon and Adam were here. Not for me, but to help look for you."

I sat next to him on the bed, forcing myself to look more calm. "Why were you hiding in the barn?"

"I didn't mean to scare you," he relented. "I didn't want to be here with just Paige and Jamie and I wasn't in the mood to hang out with my friends. I'm so sick of everyone talking about how they can't wait to get away from this place when they graduate. What's wrong with being here? With staying here?"

I knew Bryan wanted to go to a local college, but it hadn't occurred to me he didn't have the same wanderlust his sister did. How did I not know that about my own kid? "Nothing's wrong with that."

"Could've fooled me." He huffed and lay back on his bed. "I'm sorry I scared you. I don't think you're the town slut. I'll make sure to take my phone with me next time I go hide in the shed."

"Bryan..." I didn't know what to say.

He rolled on his side, back to me. "The tank was uncomfortable. I'm going to sleep."

I could dig in my heels on the punishment. Make him go clean something. Force him to stay up all day. But guilt was beating out everything else, leaving me feeling defeated.

I'd told myself for a long time that I didn't live my life based on other people's opinions, but was that true? A nagging voice in the back of my head asked if the town talking played any part in why I'd been single until now. But I had two lives I needed to be worried about. Two children I should be giving my all to. I needed to be here for Paige. For Bryan. I had to be a part of my kids' lives for as long as they needed me.

Nothing else was more important.

28
adam

WE NEED to dial things back for a while. I'm sorry.

I stared in disbelief at the text from Brooke as I sat behind the counter in Deacon's shop. We had been trying to make plans for the rest of the day when I got her message.

Dial things back. What does that mean? I replied.

Three bouncing dots taunted me as she typed. After what seemed like an eternity, but was probably only a few seconds, her message popped up.

I can't see you anymore.

No. Uh-uh. She had *not* just dumped me over text. No way. "Fuck this. I'm going back to Brooke's."

Deacon stared at me in disbelief.. "Not a good idea. She needs time to cool down."

"And I need to make things right." I showed him the brief exchange. As soon as he'd flicked his gaze over the screen then looked away, I dialed her number... and went straight to voicemail. "Brooke, what is this? Talk to me, please?" I kept my tone contrite in the message, but as soon as I hung up, my scowl was back. I hopped from the stool. "I'll be back."

I jerked to a stop when Deacon grabbed my arm and held tight. "You'll let Brooke calm down."

"Fuck you." I jerked free from his grasp and whirled to face him. "Just because you can't figure out who and what you want doesn't mean I'm going to just let someone incredible walk away."

Shit. What did I just say?

The truth.

The way Deacon watched me, his expression blank except for his clenched jaw, said he'd heard it too. "I don't know what you're talking about."

"Of course you don't." I cut off my laugh and shook my head. "And I'm not in the mood to explain it to you." I needed to figure out what was going on with Brooke. Get her back. "I'm out." I strode toward the back door.

Deacon caught up with me in the doorway that separated the main shop from the back room and grabbed my wrist.

I whirled, slammed my palm against his chest, and pressed him to the doorframe. "Don't." I bit off the word.

He gripped my arm with both hands, locking us both in place. Heat and frustration flowed between us in a potent closed circuit that threatened to fry my thoughts. "I'm definitely not letting you leave while you're like this," Deacon said.

"Why not?" This time I didn't try to pull away. I pressed in closer until we were nose-to-nose.

"Because if you go over there in this mood, you'll make things worse."

"Or maybe it's because you can't stand this. You can't stand being forced to look at what you could've had but gave up. You can't stand thinking about how emotionally stunted you are when it comes to love. You can't stand that you could've had her—me—and you don't."

Wait. What? This had never been about Deacon and me.

I was angry enough I couldn't think about it. He'd had Brooke and gave her up, and now he wanted me to do the same and I wasn't going to.

"What do you want from me?" Deacon growled.

"I want you to admit Brooke is more than just a fuck. That *I* am." With the words out there, they were real. My breath came in jagged pants and I held his gaze, refusing to look away.

Fuck. I didn't mean to say that. I didn't know I meant that.

Deacon wasn't answering. He was just watching me with the same kind of shock I felt.

Fuck it. I gripped his shirt tightly in my fist, finished closing the distance between us, and crushed my mouth to his.

He kissed back hard enough our teeth clashed. Our tongues fought. His grunts mixed with mine.

It was the middle of the day, and while we weren't exactly in front of the windows, we weren't hidden from sight either.

But the doors were locked—it wasn't like anyone was going to walk in on us, and if they caught a glimpse from outside, they were welcome to watch.

I worked my hands down the front of Deacon's shirt, ripping off as many buttons as I managed to undo in my desperation. Shoving the clothing off his shoulders left red burn marks on his skin and I followed the path with hard bites that left visible marks along his chest and shoulders.

His grunts fueled the flames raging inside me, and when he pulled my T-shirt up, I only broke away long enough to let him yank it over my head. The sound of tearing fabric added to the need flooding my veins.

I scraped my teeth over his skin and kept him pinned to the wall. He dropped his hand to grip my cock through my jeans, the friction building until I ached from the way he stroked me.

Frustration and anger and lust churned inside me until my brain didn't work and all I could think about was the man I was knotted up with. His hard body pressing into mine, the taste of his skin, of his kisses, and bringing him to his knees. Not physically. Not this time. But I wanted him to surrender to the truth.

My hips worked on their own, thrusting against the air, and shoving me into his touch.

I dragged his zipper down, and he grunted when I wrapped my fingers around his bare shaft.

I lost myself in jerking him, in the way his fingers dug into me through denim. It was pleasure and agony in a perfectly chaotic blend, until pleasure swelled to a crescendo inside me.

Deacon slammed hard against my fist, fucking as much as I was beating, and his entire body tensed. Need tightened in my balls, but I was focused on him.

When he came, it was with a loud cry, covering my hand with cum as he shuddered under my touch. His release granted me a strange satisfaction, and he never loosened his grip on me. I fucked the air. His hand. I hovered so near the edge of climax, there was no turning back.

I came hard in my jeans like I was a fucking teenager again, orgasm shuddering through my body. Pressing my hands to the wall on either side of Deacon's head, I used the sturdy structure to steady myself. To catch my breath.

We both stood there not saying anything, panting, the world moving on around us and not caring who we were. What we'd done or the mess we'd made.

The problem was, I still did. I cared who we were, and that it wasn't what we should be. That something was broken between Deacon and me, and that Brooke might as well be eons away instead of just on the other side of town.

I needed to make them both understand and I had no idea how to do that. Deacon didn't protest as I pushed away and headed toward the stairs. Fine. Fuck him. I needed to clean up.

In the bathroom, I stripped out of my clothes on auto-pilot.

The shower was too hot, but I didn't care. It washed away what was on the surface, and it seared my frustration into my soul.

I scrubbed too hard, drying myself off, and it didn't matter.

On the drive to Brooke's, my mind was a chaotic mess. The wheels on my car spun freely, looking for traction when I pulled into her driveway, and I skidded to a stop.

On her front porch, I hammered on the door with the side of my fist, until Brooke answered. Her arms were crossed, and she stared at her feet.

"Talk to me." I tried to keep my voice even.

She shook her head. "I already said what I needed to."

"No. This isn't fair. It isn't *right*." I bit the word off rather than letting it bark out. "You owe me—"

"Nothing." Brooke finally met my gaze. "I don't *owe* you anything. I can't see you anymore. That's that."

It wasn't, because it couldn't be. Was I the delusional one? No. She belonged with me. With us. "Brooke, please."

"Go home. I don't have anything else to say." Her voice cracked. She swung the door shut again before I could say more.

No. No, no, no, no, no. This wasn't the way it was supposed to be. I sank to the cold concrete of her porch, her door at my back, and dropped my head into my hands.

What was I doing wrong? Why didn't she see it? Was I the asshole here?

None of this made sense.

I lost track of how long I sat there, but enough time passed that my ass went numb. Lights flashed in the driveway and a new car pulled up next to mine.

Sebastian climbed out and approached. I watched him blankly, not able to summon a thought. He stopped in front of me. "Go home. Or anywhere but here."

"Why did she call you?"

Sebastian shrugged. "She's mad at Deacon, too? I didn't ask and whatever's going on, you're not making it better."

Yeah, apparently I *was* the asshole.

But I still didn't know what I'd done wrong, or how to fix it.

29
deacon

A<small>FTER</small> <small>THE</small> <small>SEX</small>—<small>THE</small> fucking? The mutual masturbation. I wasn't sure it could be called anything else—I let Adam shower then walk out. It wasn't like we were going to cuddle, and if he was hellbent on talking to Brooke, let him.

That didn't mean I could get his words out of my head.

I tried.

I tried to shove them out with loud music and hard labor, cranking the stereo while I worked in the basement.

He was back hours later, a scowl on his face.

I knew better than to ask how it went. I wasn't surprised, but I had hoped he'd get the answer he wanted from Brooke.

We exchanged grunts more than words as he helped me finish my work. The list wasn't long but those final touches were the things that took the most time. The basement had to look *just right*.

When we were done, we headed upstairs. I didn't have any more answers than earlier, but I'd burned off most of my frustration and was just left with exhausted confusion.

"I need another fucking shower." Adam stripped off his shirt as we walked into the apartment.

It was tempting to offer to join him, but I didn't want that to be how I knocked loose the thoughts screaming for my attention. I'd risk him using all the hot water before I did that. "You go ahead."

He studied me, his brow furrowed, then shook his head and walked into the bathroom.

I collapsed on my bed, and that gave my brain permission to assault me. To remind me how much it hurt this morning when Brooke reminded me her family wasn't mine. *My children. Not yours.*

Of course it was true, but it hurt regardless. The simple exchange tied to my past. To children I thought *were* mine. To losing a family that never really belonged to me, for the second time in my life.

And what Adam said when we got back... The accusations. The observations.

I want you to admit Brooke is more than just a fuck. That I am.

I scrubbed my hand over my barely-there hair.

What did I really want?

If I said the words, if I even thought them...

Was I prepared for the way that would change everything?

———

Monday morning didn't bring any new answers, but at least it brought the distraction of work. There was already a short line of people outside when I got downstairs, and Adam was doing some last-minute straightening.

"You posted the first video." How had I almost forgotten we were doing a soft grand-opening of the basement today? That and it was President's Day. More people always showed today, and I'd always thought buying furniture was an odd way to celebrate presidents.

Adam looked at me with his lips pursed, and his nostrils flared when he inhaled. "Of course I did. I told you I would." His tone wasn't angry, but it wasn't kind either.

"Thank you." I meant it.

We were almost ready to unlock the doors when A loud pounding came from the back of the building. I sprinted back to find out who was hammering on the door, and unlocked it to find Aubrey on the other side.

"Oh." She let out a soft huff. "It's you."

"It's my place." I was happy to see her, to talk to her, even if she hadn't said much. I hadn't changed my mind about how I felt, but I did want my friend back. "About the other night—"

She held up her index finger, silencing me. "Later. That line in front of your shop is doubling the population of the town."

"Not quite." But if things grew over the week, it might by the official grand re-opening on Saturday.

Aubrey almost smiled. "I'm hoping I see the same when Adam's video with the dresses goes live, so I'm also hoping you can have someone bring the rest of them over if you can spare a body for an hour today."

"I'll find a way."

Dylan shouted my name and I glanced back toward the main floor of the shop. Damn it, I really wanted to make things right with Aubrey.

With Adam.

With Brooke.

But Aubrey was here.

And what I had to say to Adam and Brooke reached a lot deeper into my heart, and would rip me open a lot wider.

"Go," she said. "I have a place to open too."

And that was the last thought I had about anything but antiques and how much they were worth for the next ten hours. We opened the doors at ten, locked them at seven, and haggled with stragglers until eight.

When I finally collapsed onto one of the stools behind the counter, exhaustion caught up to me. That was possibly the best day I'd ever seen this place have. People had driven in from other states. Not just Wyoming and Idaho, but Washington and Montana.

"Good day?" Aubrey's question startled me and I realized she had joined Adam and me.

"Holy shit, you scared the fuck out of me." My tired brain paused to remind me it was unusual to see her here, since she was mad at me, and that I'd forgotten to send her dresses over. "I'm so sorry. We didn't have anyone free." That was true.

"I kind of figured," she said. "That's why I'm here."

"We'll bring things over now." Adam was already on his feet.

My back ached just thinking about it—silk was a lot heavier in bulk than it looked—but Aubrey's was one door over and I owed her.

As Adam headed into the back room, I stopped Aubrey. "You have to hear me out first."

"You're going to put conditions on us doing business?" Aubrey didn't look impressed. "What are you going to say? That you're sorry for not liking me? That you still want to be friends? I get that."

I shrugged. "I'd say it more kindly than last time."

"We'll get there, D, but give me time."

It was a reasonable request. "How much time?"

Aubrey rolled her eyes. "I guess it depends on how much it hurts when I have to see you with Brooke every day."

"I'm not with Brooke." But *fuck* I wanted to be.

Now that I'd finally allowed myself to think it, the reality of how much I wanted her hit me hard.

"You guys coming?" Adam poked his head back in the room.

Or him. I wasn't with either of them, and I wanted to be. That was a jagged, bitter truth to swallow, since I'd been working so hard to make the opposite happen.

"You're such an idiot. So's she." Aubrey hopped from the stool. "Faster we get this done, faster you can go ice your back, old man."

"Give it a few days, until your lines are out the door, and see how you feel, Grandma." I fell into step beside Aubrey as we headed toward the basement.

She stuck her tongue out at me.

Over the next few days, things slowed to busy rather than hectic. Which made sense—the big antique hunters worked to get here first, and the rest would take their time. But we were putting out a bigger word on Friday, in hopes of drawing a huge crowd on Saturday.

The stream of customers didn't stop me from wondering if Travis was freaking out about the Main Street parking situation.

But more, it didn't stop me from noticing how absent Brooke was. For the third week in a row. Last weekend was supposed to mean she was back.

"Earth to Deacon." Adam's sharp whistle caught my attention. At least he was talking to me, though it had barely been about anything but business. "Dylan's taking off."

He couldn't. Not until all the customers were gone. I looked around the showroom floor. Oh. It was seven and we'd gotten everyone out. "Yeah. Okay." I shooed Dylan out and locked the doors behind him.

"Wow, a whole Thursday night to ourselves," Adam said. "Whatever will we do with our time?"

"Sleep. For a billion years." And pop some ibuprofen.

Adam shook his head. "I can give you until Saturday."

"A day and a half is like a billion years."

He snorted. "I'm so glad I don't draw a paycheck from you. I'd hate to see how you do tax deductions."

I shook my head and went to lock the front door.

Bryan slipped in before I reached my destination. Disappointment splashed inside that he was alone, but of course he was.

"What can I do for you?" I asked.

"I want a job."

Not what I expected. I turned and headed back to the counter, talking over my shoulder as I walked. I could give him the same joke I gave everyone, that I only hired people whose names started with *D*, but there was an echo in the back of my head. Brooke reminding me these were *her* kids. "I'm not hiring."

"You should be. You're busy."

It was a little petty of me to cling to her statement, but it was easier to focus on that comment than the one she never made. "Why do you want a job all the sudden? And why from me?"

"I… want to impress a girl."

"Pretty sure Paige's friend made up her mind there," Adam chimed in when we reached him.

Adam didn't like Brooke dumping him via text, but at least he got a text. Then again, I was the one who kept insisting Brooke and I were just friends. I couldn't be upset at her for my own inability to see, and that hurt.

"How do you know about that? Does everyone know?" Bryan asked.

Adam shrugged. "Paige told me. I doubt she told everyone. She's your sister—do you think she told anyone else?"

Bryan's scowl was etched deep. "No. And this isn't about Jamie."

"You can't just hop from one girl to the next." Was I talking to him or myself? I opened the register, but didn't touch the day's receipts.

Bryan made a growling noise that reminded me of Brooke when she was frustrated. "It's not like that. I'm doing the right thing. Helping her out."

"What right thing? Help her out with what?" Adam's confusion sounded exaggerated.

I wasn't sure if I should laugh or smack him.

"Nothing." Bryan shifted some things around on the counter. "Look. I'm already fitting in."

I put everything back where it had been. There was an order to these things. *Please don't make me keep a secret like this from Brooke.* Not that I could. "Does this *nothing* you're helping *a friend* out with start with a *B?*"

"Pregnancy doesn't start with— I mean, *no.*"

Yup. He'd gotten someone pregnant and that was going to be the less-than-ideal excuse I needed to call Brooke. Why did I need an excuse? I'd never needed one before.

"*Baby* starts with *B*," Adam said.

"No." Bryan sounded frustrated. "I'm not hopping from girl to girl, and it's not mine. But she is a good friend, and I can't tell you who and she doesn't want the dad to know, and her parents are going to kill her if they find out—you know how uptight some of the people here are—and she just needs to get enough money for a bus ticket to her aunt's house in Oregon. There aren't a lot of job options in this town, and you obviously need help, at least for a few days. You're sleeping with my mom, so you have to give me preference."

"*Give you preference?*" Adam repeated the oddly formal phrase.

There was a lot to unpack in this conversation. "I'm not sleeping with Brooke." Was that really what I should be focusing on right now? He was talking about helping a pregnant girl run away. "Did you not learn less than a week ago what happens when kids disappear without telling their parents?"

"Look. I need some extra cash, okay? Can we just leave it at that? Hire me for the weekend, I'll tell you

I'm spending it on comics if that helps you feel better, and it'll get you back into my mom's good graces, and maybe she'll stop moping around the house."

Something still didn't feel right about his story. Like he was working too hard to give us a tale we'd grab onto and ignore what was really happening. But I'd circle back to that, because I was hung up on the fact that Brooke was moping over us. Wait.

"Who said I was the one who needed to get back in her good graces?" I asked.

Bryan nodded at Adam. "He came to visit her almost every day while her ankle was sprained."

"Adam's on the outs too." I didn't like this direction. "Who's the money really for?"

Bryan clamped his jaw shut and shook his head.

"All right. We're going to go grab dinner." I closed the register again and turned away. "Call me when you want to give me a real answer."

"Fine, it's for Paige, okay," Bryan spit out.

Adam looked surprised. "I don't think Paige is pregnant. Do you need the birds and the bees talk?"

The look Bryan shot him was deadly. "She's only been with Jamie for a week, and she's not pregnant." He sighed. "She has a chance to apply for an apprenticeship on the other side of the country. She sent a video of her and the tank to a NASCAR pit boss, and he wants to talk to her. She has to go to the interview in person, and this is a once-in-a-lifetime chance. She could learn from NASCAR people."

"That's fantastic." This sounded more real to me. But why did it take him so long to get here?

"It is. Except"— Bryan let out another sigh— "she's terrified of going."

"How do you know?" Adam asked.

"She keeps making excuses and she made me swear on my life not to tell Mom. So Paige can't afford to go. I figure if I give her the money for the trip, she'll be out of excuses."

"And if you tell us, it gets back to Brooke." And if anyone asked, he could say we dragged the answer out of him, because we'd all but done exactly that.

Convoluted, but clever. He'd been watching way too many movies. Sounded like our kind of guy.

"You can help me clean up the shop tonight," I said. "If you call your mom and tell her where you are." I wasn't putting Brooke in a panic over a missing kid again.

Bryan rolled his eyes. "Fine." He grinned. "And thank you."

I really wanted to make things right with Brooke, and this wasn't the way to do it. Maybe I'd start with Adam and see if he was willing to forgive me for being dense, and then we'd talk to her.

Maybe.

30

brooke

"I'll be home late," Bryan said. "I'm working for Deacon now."

When I heard that name over the phone, a fist clenched around my heart, leaving an ache in its place. "Let me talk to him."

"What?" Bryan sounded surprised.

"You heard me. Put Deacon and Adam on Face-Time, so I know you're really there." And so I could hear their voices and see their faces. Mostly the first, but I hoped Bryan had learned his lesson as far as lying about where he was, so almost as much the second.

Bryan huffed. "Mom, I'm not lying."

"So put them on." If he was lying, I'd ground him for life. Maybe that was what he wanted? I didn't know anymore.

The noise on the line changed, and a heartbeat

later Bryan appeared on screen, next to Deacon, "Hi, Brooke."

"Hello." Adam was there as well.

They sounded so good. Better than should be allowed considering they hadn't said much of anything. They looked better. "Hey. Are you sure this is all right?"

"Of course." Deacon's reply came without hesitation.

"As long as he can do math," Adam said. "Apparently Deacon thinks a billion is the same as one and a half, so we need some help in the counting department."

It sounded like Deacon was clearing his throat. "I can count. One, two"—he held up fingers as he ticked off numbers, and finished with his middle finger extended, flipping off Adam—"three hundred seventy. Fuck."

Adam sucked Deacon's middle finger into his mouth, and Deacon looked like he was biting back a groan.

How did I walk away from this kind of easy fun? I didn't want to give them up, but I had kids to worry about.

And Bryan moved into the shot alone, as if to drive home the thought. "Flirt later. Boss says we have work to do."

I was certain Deacon hadn't said that, but I needed to end the call anyway. "Okay. Call if you're going to be too late."

Bryan hung up, but the teensy morsel of phone call with Adam and Deacon lingered in my thoughts and heart. I didn't like not seeing them. Not talking to them. But I also couldn't stand the thought of abandoning the twins. Making them put up with gossip. With a negligent mom.

Or I'm terrified of letting myself fall in love again.

The thought side-swiped me and I fumbled with it.

"Mom?" Paige's voice saved me from my own thoughts and I looked up to find her in the doorway of my office. "You're sitting in here alone with a dorky look on your face. Are you all right?"

"I'm fine." A little confused, but good. "What's up?"

"I need to show you something."

My heart dropped into my shoes at her hesitant tone. "Show me what?"

"Nothing bad. I hope." She stepped into my office, her voice and body language doing anything but reassuring me.

Paige pulled an empty chair closer to mine, so she was sitting next to me in front of my laptop. "So I've been trying to figure out how a tank got in our barn," she said.

It had taken her a little time to convince me she didn't move it in piece by piece, but I did believe her now.

"I can't find much of anything except that the man who owned this place before us, his grandfather brought it home at the end of World War I. There are photos of it arriving on the train."

It was a strange story that left me with more questions than answers, but it didn't explain the way she was acting. "Okay?"

"But while I was looking... Can I?" She nodded at my computer.

I rolled out of the way to give her access.

Paige moved in, and her fingers flew across the keyboard. She opened several tabs, and I caught a glimpse of each, most of the pages looking like basic, early internet days sites. The kind with busy backgrounds and lots of text.

"I know why Deacon has a basement, and why there's that stuff in it," she said. "His great, great grandparents owned a lot more of that block when the city was founded. And, well..." Paige gestured at the screen she'd stopped on.

The Unbelievably True Story of Utah's First Brothel

I stared in disbelief at the headline. "No way."

"I did a lot of cross referencing"—she gestured at the other tabs—"and it looks like it's true. They opened it for miners, and the state shut it down, boarded it up, and made them surrender most of the street-level property."

"Wow." I scrolled through the page, skimming every third word—enough to pick up the meaning—this is... *wow*."

"Right?" Paige sounded excited. "You're fucking someone who owns a part of sex history."

"I'm not…" *fucking him*. I sighed. I wanted to be. I wanted to be more with Deacon. I wanted to go back to Adam. Why did I push them away?

"Why not?" Paige's question echoed my thoughts.

Because of her and Bryan?

Because I was scared.

There was that thought again, and this time I couldn't shake it. "I don't know."

Paige sank lower in her seat. "I get that."

But the idea of pushing past this fear brought so many arguments. Deacon had already balked at the idea of more. More than once. There was no reason for him to change his mind.

But Adam had plenty of reasons that all went back to him realizing there was so much more out there than me for him.

It was a lot less painful to tell myself I was keeping my distance for the twins' sake.

I looked back at the various sites Paige had pulled up on my computer, about Deacon's building. There was something I could do that had nothing to do with sex or romance.

Okay, it had a lot to do with sex, but not sex with me.

I didn't suspect that having a place declared a historical site was as easy as they made it on TV, but I was going to figure it out.

I spent the next several hours learning everything I could about the process, and didn't go to bed until my eyes were too dry to make sense of words anymore. Friday morning I was back at it, including calling in a favor with a friend who worked at our town hall, to help me answer some questions on the paperwork.

Turning onto Main Street filled me with a mix of nervous anticipation and dread, from memories of every time I'd come down here to visit the antique shop, and knowing I wasn't going there today.

I parked out of sight of their shop windows, mostly because I was a Grade A coward and would cave and make a fool of myself if I ran into either man. I wasn't thinking about the fact that I'd have to go talk to them after this, to share the good news. Instead, I cut through the back alley across the street.

As I drew closer to the City building, a strange noise caught my attention, and I paused. Grunting? No. Not when I strained. Murmuring. Like voices. Definitely.

It wasn't polite to eavesdrop, but curiosity won out. I followed the sound toward two buildings with a barely-there gap between them, and found two men with a barely there gap between them. Their foreheads were pressed together, one with his hands resting at the base of the other's neck as they muttered words I couldn't make out.

"Travis?" His name slipped past my lips before I could stop it.

They both looked up, startled.

"Oh, crap." The younger man paled when he saw

me, and sprinted off in the other direction without another word.

I knew him, as well. Manny was the current bishop's oldest son. He was also barely twenty-two, and had just gotten back from a church mission in Uruguay.

For the most part, I didn't care what anyone did with anyone else, as long as it was consensual, but given the grief Travis had tossed at me over the years —the self-righteous, snotty, gossipy bullshit—it was hard not to act smug right now.

"Don't say anything." Travis strode toward me. His strong tone was in sharp contrast to the fact that his eyes darted in every direction. "You've been with younger men, too."

I could play the *but I'm a woman* card, but really that felt slimy. Even now. "I have. And thank you for telling the entire town about that, by the way."

"You can't keep something like that a secret."

Was he really trying to make this about me? No thank you. "You're right, you can't." It was so tempting to rake him over the coals with this, but I wasn't him. I did have one issue with what I'd seen though—I couldn't help but wonder how I'd feel if it was one of my kids, barely older than they were now, with a manipulative, cruel asshole who was Travis's age. "Big difference is, Adam and Deacon are only a few years younger than me, not nearly two decades. This will get out. You know that, don't you?"

"Are you threatening me?"

Adam would've drawn a Beavis comparison at this point. I missed him. "No. I'm not a gossip. I'm telling you how it is. If I caught you, someone else will." Though it was so tempting to shout this from the rooftops. Was I a good enough person to keep it to myself?

Manny didn't deserve the whispers, even if Travis should be subjected to much worse.

"Why are you here?" Travis asked.

Not a great attempt to redirect the conversation, but not bad. "Not to talk to you. In fact, I have an appointment in"—I checked my watch—"two minutes. I need to go."

"Wait." Travis grabbed my arm.

I shot him a withering glare and he let go.

"Please don't tell anyone about this." The strength was gone from his voice.

I didn't plan on it, so I gave him a shrug.

"What are you meeting about? What can I help with? Anything. You name it."

Was Travis going through the seven stages of getting caught? Were we on bargaining? I had no idea what came next. "I'm having this block declared a historic site, which means you can't force the stores to make changes."

He went paler—so that was possible—and worked his jaw up and down, a bit like a fish gasping in air. "They're good plans, Brooke. I just want this block to look gorgeous."

"This block is already amazing. How do you not

see that? We're not like other Main Streets with half the shops boarded up and the other half trying to pretend they're modern. We sparkle and shine."

Travis scoffed. "Great. I'll have you write the marketing brochures."

"And I need to go."

"Wait. Please." Sweet-Travis was back. "What if I promise you right now I'll get the new requirements reversed. No changes."

"I'm about to do that anyway, and honestly your word isn't worth crap."

"I won't fight it. I'll step aside right now, just don't tell anyone what you saw."

"Over a guy?" I didn't believe that. Then again, I'd give up a lot for Adam and Deacon. I was an idiot for giving them up. Besides, I didn't care that Travis wanted to screw men, I just cared that the one he picked was so young, and Travis was so fucking manipulative.

"If this gets out, my career…" Travis gave me a look that said *don't make me finish this thought*.

"You'll be screwed in a whole new way. I really need to keep going."

"I'll walk you in." Travis fell into step beside me.

I couldn't stop him from walking where he wanted to, and it felt wrong to manipulate this situation to my advantage, especially since I didn't plan to tell anyone what I saw. But was there really any harm in letting Travis continue to believe everyone in the world was the same kind of asshole he was?

But was I really that much better than him? He was keeping his relationship quiet, and I was so scared of my relationships that I'd ended them before they got off the ground.

I was tired of making excuses about why I couldn't be with Deacon and Adam. It was time for me to step up. To go after them, regardless of what the rest of the world thought about us.

31
adam

DEACON and I were discussing the pros and cons of closing the shop right after lunch, to spend the second half of Friday getting ready for the Official Basement Grand Opening, when Bryan walked into the shop.

"Shouldn't you be in school?" I wasn't up for keeping any more secrets from Brooke.

He didn't look bothered by the question. "Nope. Fridays I get half a day for college courses in Salt Lake, but those were canceled. So I'm here for more work."

"You can't just set your own schedule," Deacon said.

"I'm taking initiative. Besides, Paige is on a timer, even if she won't admit it."

Hard to argue with that.

Deacon grabbed his keys. "Right. We're closing early, and Bryan can start bringing the rest of the clothing over to Aubrey's."

For the next couple of hours, we worked without much conversation beyond Deacon's direction. The manual labor was exhausting, but it was a different kind of tiring than dealing with people who wanted everything for nothing, like we'd seen so many times this week.

Some days I didn't know how Deacon put up with it, but he loved it, and I loved watching him do it.

I loved…

Yeah, I did.

"Hey." Bryan interrupted the thought. "What's with the dopey look?"

I'd linger on love later. "I'm just lucky—I have a naturally dopey face. Aren't you moving end tables?"

"Pft. I'm going. Slave driver." Bryan's tone was light as he walked away.

"You're the one who wanted a job," Deacon called after him.

Deacon had a handful of *full room* setups around the shop, similar to what one would find in a furniture store. He set up the displays to keep sets together or to show how mismatched sets could work together, and he tended to rotate them out every so often.

The exception to the rule was the set Bryan had stopped next to. "This has been here for a while, hasn't it? We could swap it out."

This was one of the matching sets, from the pair of antique cribs to the matching dressers and wooden rocker. The set never moved. Deacon had refused every offer on it, regardless of price or whether the person wanted one piece or the whole set.

"*No*." Deacon's bark came out of nowhere.

I knew why, but that didn't mean the response was warranted, and Bryan's surprised expression said he agreed. "Okay. We won't move it," Bryan said.

"Sorry," Deacon muttered. "The set stays. We'll move other things."

It had been so many years, and that wound was still fresh for Deacon. I got it, though. There were days when memories of my dad still hit me like he's just been here yesterday.

The silence that settled in was stifling.

"Was it ours?" Bryan asked out of nowhere.

Deacon stared at him. "What?"

"You're in love with my mom, right? Widow moves to town with two kids, she needs a place to hawk some of their old stuff—"

"It's not yours." Deacon's tone had gone from over the top angry to almost mechanical. "And I didn't own the shop when Brooke moved here."

There was no denial of *I'm not in love with her*. Not that I could blame him—some lies were hard to keep up. I was willing to admit I loved Brook as much as I did Deacon, and with any luck, he'd figure it out soon too.

"Your family did." Either Bryan couldn't read a room, or he was enjoying pushing Deacon's buttons.

Deacon shrugged. "Not sure what your point is."

My phone chirped with a text message from my brother. It read, *I'm here*.

"Brandon's out back to pick up the lights," I said. "Saved by the bell," I muttered quietly enough only Deacon should hear me.

Deacon rolled his eyes. "Whatever."

Whatever indeed. I wouldn't push the issue, especially in front of other people, but I would like it if he opened up to me at some point.

As we loaded the borrowed lights into Brandon's SUV, Deacon had gone quiet, most likely lost in the past, with the memories that belonged to that furniture set.

There were so many times when Deacon had pulled me out of a funk over the course of our friendship—after fights with Brandon, after my ex left, when my business partner torched my plans and my home, on the anniversary of my dad's death...

Deacon was always there for me, and as soon as everyone left today, I was going to make sure he had whatever he needed, whether that was talking, silence, or sex. Was the last one an unhealthy outlet for grief? Probably. But I'd do a lot for him.

"Hey, you ever see that really old movie, Aliens?" Bryan asked, as we finished loading the last of the gear into Brandon's SUV, and closed the doors.

Brandon's snort was one I'd heard too many times in my life. It was *you can't be serious right now*.

I had a similar response, but with a very different

emotion behind it. "I can't believe you just asked me that."

"So, yes?" Bryan said.

"I'm ready, man, check it out," I shouted in my best Hudson voice, quoting a specific scene from *Aliens* special edition. "State of the art badass art. You do not want to fuck with me."

Bryan grinned. "Hey, Ridley, don't worry." He looked at Brandon. "Me and my squad of ultimate badasses will protect you. Check it out—independently targeting particle beam phalanx."

"*Vwap.*" I added the sound effects. "Fry half a city with this puppy."

Bryan picked it up again without pause. "We got tactical smart missiles, phased plasma pulse rifles, RPGs, and sonic electronic ball breakers."

I joined in at the end, and we spoke at the same time. "We got nukes, knives, sharp sticks—"

"Knock it off, Hudson." Deacon slapped my arm lightly.

"What's the relevance here?" Brandon didn't look impressed.

Deacon laughed. "If you don't get it, there's no reason to explain it."

"This is totally Movie-ception." And I was here for it. "I can be the Tony Stark to Bryan's Peter Parker."

Brandon raised an eyebrow. "*That* reference I get, and you are *not* Tony Stark."

Ouch. "Why not?"

"You're sexier." Deacon to the rescue.

Allyson Lindt

"Not as arrogant," Bryan added. "Or old."

Brandon clapped me on the arm. "Smarter."

That made me feel better.

We left Deacon and Bryan to work and I took Brandon on a tour of the basement, and couldn't help but beam when he told me it looked great. I didn't put a lot of stock into most people's opinions, but this was my big brother, no matter how old we got.

There was a teensy, tiny bit of me that wished he'd give me this kind of praise for my creative work, but I was a big boy, I could suck that up.

When we were done, I walked him outside.

"Hey, I've seen the videos on your channel. The new ones." His voice was casual as we paused inside the back doorway.

I swore I stopped breathing ."Yeah?"

"They look really good. You deserve the traffic you're getting, and more."

I couldn't help the smile that broke out across my face. "Thank you."

"I have something for you,"

"Is it in the car?" I liked presents.

"No." He reached in his pocket.

I couldn't help myself. "It's inappropriate for me to make a joke about pockets and presents, isn't it? Since you're my brother and all?"

"Don't know when that's ever stopped you." He pulled out two earbud cases and handed one to me. He always carried a second set, sterilized and paired to his phone. Some people were put off by it, but I was used to it. He was a composer and this was how he liked to share music.

I slipped the buds in my ears, curious, and Brandon did the same.

Brandon played me a thirty-second or so clip that was a catchy, fast tempo, rock tune.

"I like it," I said. "Of course I do. Is it the intro to something?"

"Your channel. If you want it, that is. I can tweak it."

He'd written custom music for me? "It's awesome. It's amazing. It's perfect."

Brandon chuckled. "I'll send you the file. Give it a few more listens and make sure, then let me know."

"Thank you. I mean it—thank you." I was being a dork. I didn't care.

The hinges on the back door creaked, and when Brooke walked in, I forgot everything else. Rude of me, but she was here, watching me with a shy smile, looking more stunning than I remembered. I didn't care that it hadn't even been a week, I couldn't pull my gaze from her..

"I'm gonna go." Brandon's voice barely penetrated my thoughts.

"So soon?" My protest didn't have any force behind it.

"I see that look on Danny all the time. I wear it a lot myself. You don't want me here right now."

I really didn't. "Thank you."

"For not being a cock block?"

Brooke flushed at Brandon's question.

I laughed. "For everything."

Brandon left, but I was still watching Brooke.

"Hey," Brooke said softly. Her voice was lyrical. "Is this a good place to talk?"

Maybe later it would be. I didn't have the words for what I needed her to know. I cupped her face in my palms, and pressed my body and mouth to hers, pushing into her until her back hit the wall.

She gasped into the kiss, and I stole the chance to dart my tongue into her mouth and devour her sighs. She gripped my shirt in her fists and held me close. Not that I planned on going anywhere.

Brooke was a lifeline and I'd been drowning without her and had refused to admit it. I nipped at her lips and licked along her skin and held on for dear life.

"I don't care," I said breathlessly. "I don't care what it takes. I want you, I need you, and I'm never letting you go."

"I don't want you to."

Her lips were already swollen, and my nipping at them made them puffier and softer and if possible, more kissable. "Good." I dragged my thumbs along her cheekbones. "Because I love you. I'm desperately and completely and hopelessly in love with you and I'm not letting you go." *But...* I worked my jaw.

"But what?" Brooke asked, despite the fact I didn't speak the word aloud.

I wasn't sure I should say. This was so close to

perfect, but I wanted it all, and I had to try. "Keep that in mind, how very much I love you."

"You're going to have to finish the thought eventually." Her tone was light.

I could call on the lack of her saying it back, but I wouldn't force that. "But I love Deacon too. I want you both. He doesn't know that. I wasn't sure I knew it until just now."

"Me too," Brooke said. "That's why I'm here."

This time my kisses were more gentle. "That's a cop-out. You have to actually say what you're agreeing with."

"I love you too. Even though it hasn't been long, not talking to you destroyed me. I can't imagine not having you in my life." She leaned her weight into me. "But Deacon... I want him there too."

I let out an exaggerated sigh. "I can only see one solution for our future."

Brook looked worried. "What's that?"

"We're going to have to tell him he's ours."

She laughed lightly. "That sounds perfect."

It really did. And I saw a whole lot more perfect in our future—all three of us could take on the world if we had to, and if we didn't, we'd still have each other.

And there really was no better word for that than *perfect*.

32

deacon

WHILE ADAM AND BRANDON TALKED, I was doing some last-minute work with Bryan on the main showroom floor, moving some items forward that I felt needed more eyes on them.

The conversation about the twins' cribs stuck in my thoughts, attached to the past and refusing to budge.

"What did you do that made Mom push you out?" Bryan's question came out of nowhere.

I didn't want to have this conversation with him, or think about the answers myself. "Nothing." From one perspective, that was true.

"If it had to do with me, with last Sunday, I'm sorry. I didn't think that would be the big deal it became. I figured I'd tell Paige I was at a friend's, I'd go take some time to think, and I'd be back before anyone questioned it."

That was a messy day, and Brooke's reminder lingered with me that her family wasn't mine. But of course it wasn't—the realization slammed into me. I'd made sure it was never an option. "It wasn't your fault, it was mine."

"You said you didn't do anything." Bryan stared me down.

"I never gave her a chance to reject me." The words were meant more for me than him. "I made damn sure that wasn't up to her."

Bryan shifted his weight and jammed his hands in his pockets. "That's messed up."

"It really is." I was making him uncomfortable. "Anyway, that's that." And it was up to me to fix that mistake. Because it was a massive mistake—pushing Brooke away. Adam. I didn't know how I was going to make things right. "It was for my kids. The bedroom set." Why did I say that?

Bryan looked surprised. "You have kids?"

"No." I could keep this story simple. Free of emotion. "Years ago, just a little after you all moved to town, I was dating a girl who was pregnant. Twins." I'd been so excited to have a family. "Turned out they weren't mine, and she left me for their father."

"Ouch."

I had no idea where to go from here. I was spilling my secrets to a teenager. Why? I should tell him to get back to work and do the same. Maybe go see what Adam was up to.

"I barely remember my dad," Bryan's voice was quiet. "Some days I wonder if that makes me a bad person."

"You weren't very old when you lost him."

"Old enough. Even though you didn't get to raise those kids, you would've. You were there, ready and willing. That counts for a lot."

I needed to change topics fast, but I couldn't wrap my brain around a smooth transition. "You're not a bad person. You're doing so much for your family. It's obvious you love them." *Stop now.* This was the perfect place to wrap up this conversation.

"But I get it. I do." Apparently I was still talking. "My dad walked out when I was five. Left me with his parents and never came back. I wondered for a long time if that was my fault, and the more time that passed, the more he faded from my mind, the more I blamed myself."

And that, combined with the bad experience in my twenties, *losing* kids I'd looked forward to raising, made me pull away. At least I had the presence of mind to not share that revelation, but it knocked my mind off kilter regardless.

"You would've been a good dad," Bryan said.

I didn't know if he was just saying that, but it warmed me regardless. "You *are* a good son."

"So, I'll check back with you tomorrow morning. Grand opening and all that. I need my rest." Bryan's words tumbled out in a rush.

What the hell?

I was even more confused when he hurried out the door. So much for that touching moment.

"It's not you, it's us." Adam's voice from behind startled me.

I spun to see him standing in the doorway to the back room, his arm around Brooke.

"No one wants their mom to see them getting all sappy," she said.

Right. They were talking about Bryan. I didn't care, because my heart was cracking, seeing them together. I didn't care if Adam said I wasn't allowed to feel that way—I did. I hated seeing them together and not being a part of it, and it had taken me a long time to own that feeling, but here it was. "How much did you hear?"

"The last couple of minutes." Adam dropped his hand to capture Brooke's, and tugged her to fall into step beside him as they strolled toward me.

"It's a shame he ran out like that," Brooke said. "He's going to miss the good news."

Something told me he didn't want to hear me pouring my heart out to his mom. Telling both Brooke and Adam how I really felt and doing whatever it took to get them to give me a real chance. "My news first."

Brooke shook her head. "Mine won't take long, but you do need to hear it. I'm having the block declared a historic site."

"What?" Adam's surprise overlapped mine. "You didn't think to mention that back there?"

Brooke blushed. "One, Deacon needed to hear it first, and two, my mouth was full."

I didn't know if I was too stunned about her news to be jealous. No, I did know. I was still furiously envious that Adam had already claimed her again. They seemed to be all better. "How?" I asked.

Brooke explained what Paige found, and my surprise grew until my eyes were probably as wide as saucers—I finally understood what that meant. "Travis signed the paperwork just a short while ago, halting the requirements the council had put on the block. No one has to make the changes, even though my application is still being processed."

"That's amazing. Holy shit." I didn't have enough words to convey how excited I was about the news, but Brooke looked like she was holding something back. "What aren't you telling us? How did you get Travis to back down?"

"I uh… I ran into him on my way to the city building. Making out with Manny in a back alley."

My jaw dropped. "No shit." Not as surprising as the rest of her news, but still not something I consciously thought I'd ever hear.

"I tried to tell him I wasn't a gossip, but I know he yielded to get me to keep quiet about what I saw," Brooke said.

I'd keep the information to myself as well, and the

other news was so good. But my gaze kept drifting back to the way Adam and Brooke's fingers were tangled together.

It was my fault that I wasn't with her. That I'd never taken a chance to tell her I wanted more, because I never admitted it to myself, and now that she was with Adam… "I'm going to be that asshole," I said.

Adam raised his brows. "Not new."

"As opposed to the other asshole?" Brooke asked. "The secondary one most people don't talk about?"

"Clever." I was dryly amused.

"Almost always." Adam squeezed Brooke's hand.

The two of them were distracting in the best way, even now. "Let me get this out."

"That's what she said?" Brooke grinned.

I laughed. "I need to be serious for maybe sixty seconds, and then you can make jokes again."

Adam looked like he was struggling to keep a straight face.

I sighed. "Get it out."

"That's sooo long." He dragged out the words.

"That's what she said." Brooke's grin grew.

This was already going to be difficult, but I needed to say it now, because I refused to lose them. I wouldn't surrender the family I'd always wanted, and missed when it was right in front of me. "The two of you can't be together without giving me a chance."

Adam opened his mouth.

"With both of you." I had to keep going, or I'd never get this out. "You have to give me a chance to be a part of what you have with each other. I was an idiot, not admitting to myself how I felt. Pushing Brooke away. Pretending I didn't love Adam. I do. I love you Adam, and Brooke as well. I wish I could be more eloquent about it, but—"

Adam dropped Brooke's hand and gripped the back of my neck, stealing my voice. He kissed me hard and drew out the moment until everything fell away except the three of us.

I pushed him back, needing to say just a little more, but I couldn't find the words.

"We were all idiots." Adam's voice was gravel. "But I love you too, and I'm so fucking glad you figured it out. Though I wouldn't have minded a little more hate sex first."

"There was hate sex? And I missed it?" Brooke pouted.

"I'll give you something much better." I stepped away from Adam and wrapped an arm around Brooke's waist. "I don't know why it took me so long to own this, but I've been infatuated with you since the first day I saw you, and I don't know when it became more, but the way I love you now is so intense it consumes me."

"I love you too. So much it scares me. But I finally figured out you're worth the risk. You both are. You're going to let me keep Adam too. I assume."

I glanced at Adam, and he beamed. "You know neither of you could really give me up."

"It's true." And I was finally willing to own that fact.

Adam gripped the back of my neck with both hands, and I mimicked the gesture, our mouths clashing then molding together in a kiss that sealed me to him. How did I ignore what I felt for him for so long?

I didn't want to let him go, but I wanted Brooke, too. I reluctantly broke away from Adam, and turned to Brooke. "I've wanted to do this for so long," I said.

Brooke's questioning look, from her lightly furrowed brow to the seductive slant of her lips, amplified my desire.

I glided my fingers lightly along her jaw, to her neck, and finally to grip her hair tightly in my fist. Her gasp sent desire spilling through me. I yanked hard, and captured her mouth, swallowing her moan.

How did I pretend for so long that my feelings for her, for Adam, were anything less than this intense need? I wanted to kiss Brooke from now until eternity. She was my lifeline and my breath and my universe.

I forced myself to break away, but I know I couldn't keep my mouth off her for long. "I really want to take you in front of these giant windows." My voice was ragged. "But we should probably not."

"It's going to happen eventually." Adam had a good point.

Brooke's eyes grew wide. "Would you—we—really do that?"

"Fuck in front of the picture windows?" I liked the idea a *lot*. "If you're interested."

She nodded. "Not tonight, but yeah, I think I could be convinced."

It was going on the list.

"I'm going to need so many more lessons." Brooke sounded as excited as the words made me feel.

Adam wrinkled his nose. "Can we not call them that?"

"I like *list*." One was growing in my head with each suggestion and innuendo. "I've already got a good-sized one of things I'd like to do to you."

"Just me?" Brooke glanced sideways. "What about Adam?"

I shrugged, trying to look more casual than I felt. Truly, I wanted all the things from both of them. "I've already done a lot of them with Adam, so he can watch." Teasing slid into my reply.

Adam raised his brows. "I'm only content to watch sometimes."

"Like now?" Brooke's question lilted up.

She must've *really* liked the fucking-in-front-of-the-window idea.

"Let's start there," Adam said. "But only because I've had fantasies about watching Deacon ravage you for a long time."

He had? Fucking. Hot.

The three of us trekked upstairs, and I steered Brooke into my room.

Adam stepped back, and the way his heated gaze followed us would've had me hard if I wasn't already sporting a steel rod in my pants.

I was intently aware of our audience of one while I took my time stripping down Brooke. I pulled her shirt off first, covering her neck and shoulders in kisses. Then I removed her bra. There was no need to hurry, and I couldn't have even if there was a time limit. I wanted to savor her breasts and taste her nipples and suck until she was whimpering and fisting my shirt and squirming under my attention.

When I finally moved on, I slid her jeans and panties down her legs, stripped her shoes off, and the rest of her clothing. Standing, I claimed her mouth again and slipped my hand between her legs.

She was wet with anticipation. My fingers glided easily along her skin to part her folds. She bucked against my touch when brushed over her clit.

I dropped my head to her breast again, sucking while I circled her swollen button. The delicious sounds that tore from her chest spurred me on. I fingered and teased, and she squeezed her legs together and rocked against my touch.

When her body started to shake, I knew she was close. I pushed in harder, coaxing her into orgasm. Reveling in her screams of pleasure.

She pulled away with a soft laugh. "Too much."

"Do you want to stop?" I'd fuck Adam, but I'd rather have more of her as well.

Brooke shook her head. "No. I just need a breather."

"Good. Because I want to feel both of you at the same time," I said.

"I'm not sure I understand."

I held up my index finger. "Me." I extended my middle finger so the two were together. "And Adam. Inside you." I slipped my fingers inside her.

33
brooke

I UNDERSTOOD what Deacon was proposing, but I wasn't sure it was possible. Still, I was so turned on, and so hungry to feel both men at once, I was definitely going to give it a try. "All right."

At my agreement, Adam stepped forward to join us. I lost track of hands, but not kisses as they both crushed their mouths to mine and each other's. They stripped their clothes away between gropes and bites.

I loved watching them together as much as feeling them with me. Their passion was obvious—the same sparks that made me think for so long that they were already a couple. There was no denying how well they fit together, or how lucky I was to be a part of this. Of them.

When they stood naked next to me, shafts at attention and the hunger in their eyes making me feel like I was a delicious part of the meal, they rolled on condoms.

Deacon pressed his body to mine, and his erection dug into my stomach. I could melt into him like this, especially when Adam molded his chest to my back and nipped at my neck. He sneaked his head past mine to kiss Deacon, turning me into the yummy filling on their sandwich.

This entire experience was a whole new level of *wow*.

With his hands on my hips, Deacon slid back onto the bed and coaxed me to join him. "Straddle me," he said as he laid back.

I tried to be sexy, climbing up his legs, but I was pretty sure I didn't pull it off. "Is there a way to do this and not look awkward?"

"The first day I met you, I couldn't stop thinking about how sexy you were. I've never been able to take my eyes off you." Deacon's warm assurance washed over me.

Heat flooded my cheeks. "I always thought you were teasing me. When you said, well, most anything about how I looked."

Adam sighed. "I told you."

"I know." Deacon pursed his lips. "I was too much of a coward to just tell you how I felt. You're so... you."

I had no idea what that meant. "Is that good?"

Adam kissed along my shoulder. "That's incredible."

"*You're* incredible." Deacon slipped his palms up

my thighs, toward the source of my need. He guided me onto him and slid inside me, stretching me out in the most delicious way. The groan he made was another delicious touch fluttering over me.

I still had no idea how this was supposed to work. Just Deacon was enough to make me wince—in a good way, but still.

A new touch slipped over my skin from behind, as Adam liberally applied lube, then coaxed his fingers into me.

"Relax." Adam's voice was low and comforting. It still made my pulse hammer against my ribs, knowing what he was going to try next.

He took his time teasing and stretching my opening with his fingers, and then when he slipped his shaft inside me. The sensation was almost too much, but it also felt incredible.

Both men rested there, cock to cock, cradling me between them. Adam slipped his hands forward to find my clit. To tease the button still swollen and sensitive from Deacon's touch. Adam stroked until climax built under my skin. Until I was riding the edge of orgasm, but not falling over. I was clenching around them, my body not sure if the sensations were good or bad.

When pleasure rushed through me, it was like a dam had broken. I dug my fingers into Deacon's arms, losing track of myself when I came. I pressed back into both of them.

This sensation was different, borderline uncomfortable, but so incredible.

Before the sensation faded, both men started rocking against each other. Deacon pulled me into him, and wrapped his lips around a nipple. Adam gripped my hips tightly. They both hit spots inside me I didn't know existed.

Was this a series of orgasms, or one long, drawn-out one?

I didn't care. It felt so good. So easy to lose myself in all of it, until the world ceased to exist.

Adam and Deacon were both making those incredible noises I associated with them finishing. Grunts and growls and drawn-out groans. Together they were a delicious chorus, and I wasn't sure which of them finished first.

The frantic thrusting slowed to a stop. There was pain when Adam pulled out of me, but I'd do this again in a heartbeat. So worth it.

Deacon slipped out as well.

The mattress shifted and Adam wrapped his arms around my waist, holding me against him. His hot breath hit the back of my neck as he caught his breath.

Deacon cradled my face, and kissed my forehead, then my nose, and finally my lips. "Don't go home tonight."

"I won't." There was no way I could force myself from their arms.

For so long, I'd told myself the twins needed me to be their world. I never minded giving them everything I could, but after I lost my husband I assumed I had to do it alone. As my kids grew closer to *leave the nest* age, I'd assumed I would be alone.

But I didn't have to be. It was okay for me to love and live and pursue amazing opportunities, and I wasn't depriving them of anything.

And falling asleep in Adam's and Deacon's arms was okay. It was better than okay. It was amazing.

When I woke up, for a brief moment I was terrified that last night, the *I love yous* were a dream, but when I felt Adam and Deacon wrapped around me, I could breathe again. I had them. This was all real.

The day passed in a blur, as Deacon opened to more people than I'd ever seen in his shop, and kept busy all day. The rest of us didn't know the antiques the way he did, but we could take money, load furniture, and move things around as needed.

By the time he locked the front doors, almost two hours after the store was supposed to close, we were all exhausted. But it was in a good way.

We were discussing how to spend the rest of the night, and talking about sending Dylan and Bryan home, when Sebastian stopped by. Then Evie and Aubrey and a few other people who owned shops on the block.

"Is the rumor true?" Evie asked.

Deacon gave her a blank look. "Rumor?"

"That Brooke talked Travis out of that bullshit he was trying to force down our throats," Sebastian said.

Adam grinned. "Oh yeah, that's totally true." He

slid up behind me and the stool I was sitting on behind the counter, and rested his hands on my hips.

"I think this calls for a celebration." Aubrey pulled a bottle of champagne from the large purse hanging from her shoulder.

I was impressed. "Do you carry that with you everywhere?"

"The purse? Yes. The champagne? No, but I had a feeling if anyone could pull something like this off, it would be Brooke."

"Hey." Deacon sounded hurt. "Why her and not me?"

Aubrey sighed and shrugged. "Because sometimes you're kind of dumb."

Deacon stuck his tongue out at her.

I grabbed his hand and pulled him back to stand closer to us. "Dumb, but really pretty."

"That's true," Adam said.

Deacon huffed. "Not sure if I'm offended or not."

Evie raised her brows. "You're not sure if you'd rather be pretty or smart? Seriously?"

"Let's eat, drink, and celebrate the amazing news and the business this is bringing in." Sebastian grabbed the bottle from Aubrey.

The party moved into full swing. I fielded *thank yous* from most everyone as the night went on. Deacon or Adam or both of them were by my side most of the night, and it became apparent Aubrey was avoiding one of us.

She approached me when I found myself alone. "Thank you for making this possible," she said.

"I had to. You all deserve it." I'd been saying a variation on the same thing most of the night and I still meant it.

Aubrey shifted her weight to her other foot and started to turn away, but turned back to me again. "You're lucky, you know."

"In a lot of ways."

"I mean to have Deacon. And I'm glad someone good is going to take care of him."

I wasn't sure how to respond to that besides *I know*, and that didn't seem like the right answer. "Screw that. He'd better take care of me. I'm old." I hid a wince at the self-depreciation.

"You're not old," Aubrey said.

A pair of hands slid around my waist and I knew without looking that Adam had appeared out of nowhere. "She's right, you're not."

"Not what?" Deacon had joined us too.

Aubrey's expression shifted toward blank, but she didn't leave. "Not old."

"Definitely not." He grasped my fingertips.

We'd spent the night acting like the three of us were together, but it hadn't hit me how little we'd done to hide it until Aubrey's gaze dropped to my hand in Deacon's. The three of us, Adam, Deacon, and I were official, and the more I thought about it, the more I loved it.

When more people were yawning than talking, we sent everyone home, shut off the lights, and agreed to clean up the pizza boxes and plastic cups around the trash can in the morning.

The three of us headed upstairs. I should go home at some point, but Bryan and Paige had promised they were okay alone for another night.

I was just glad they were talking again.

"What's on your mind?" Adam asked softly.

So many things, I wasn't sure I could put them all into words. But I was willing to try. "When I moved here years ago, it was to get away from everything that reminded me of my husband, and because I wanted the twins to grow up somewhere sane. In a close-knit community. Except, I didn't find the kind of closeness I was looking for—not as it applied to me, anyway. I stuck it out for them, and there were so many days I wondered if I was doing the right thing."

"They turned out pretty good, so I'd say *yes*." Deacon's voice was soft and kind.

"So did you," Adam added.

Deacon shook his head. "I disagree."

What? "You do?"

Deacon kissed the tip of my nose. "You turned out the perfect amount of bad."

"Touché," Adam said.

"And that's good?" I was pretty sure it must be, but I had to be positive.

Adam took both our hands. "It's perfect."

He was right, it really was. I never could've imagined this life for myself, and now that I had it, I couldn't imagine being happier. This was better than any fairytale. This was my perfect happy ending.

epilogue

Brooke

one year later

I SHOULD BE USED to this by now, but it was still a novelty to me to be sitting at my own kitchen table while Adam made breakfast. I was sipping my coffee, enjoying the morning, and he was wearing an apron the twins got me years ago that said *World's Best Mom*, while he dipped and flipped French toast on the electric griddle.

"Is everyone decent?" Paige's call came from the next room.

Adam chuckled and shook his head.

"We're clothed, I promise," I replied.

Paige had been in Florida for the last few months, learning the basics of sport car repair from the NASCAR team she was working for. Starting in a week or so, she'd be going on tour with them, so they gave her a few days off.

She decided to surprise me with the news, and walked in on Deacon, Adam, and me making out in the living room. Fortunately no clothes had come off completely yet, but she insisted she was scarred for life.

Paige walked in and took the seat next to me.

Adam set a plate of food in front of her.

"Nice apron." Paige's teasing was light and friendly.

"Thanks." He grinned. "It's all true. Nice shirt."

Paige looked down at the graphic that said *Professional Fish Taco Eater* and returned his smirk. "Thanks."

When Jamie's parents found out she was dating Paige, they'd kicked her out. Jamie stayed with us for a while, but she and Paige had an apartment in Orlando now. Jamie was working at Walt Disney World and loving it.

I was grateful Paige didn't care what people thought, that she was even willing to flaunt her opinion in shirt form, because people in town talked *a lot* about my relationship with Deacon and Adam.

The other shop owners on Main Street supported us, though. I'd gotten closer to most of Deacon's neighbors, especially Aubrey now that she and Deacon were friends again.

Paige, Adam, and I were halfway through breakfast when the sound of the front door opening reached me, and Bryan called, "*hello*."

"In here," Paige yelled back.

I winced and mimed clearing out my ear.

Bryan rented a room from Sebastian. He'd moved out at the start of the college school year because he wanted to stay in town, but he didn't want to admit his mom had sex. Those were his words. *I don't care if you date two men, but I don't want to admit you have sex.*

"Food?" Paige held up her plate.

Bryan pulled up an empty seat. "Already ate. We ready to do this?"

"I'll go wake up Deacon." Adam finished his breakfast and stood.

Normally we let Deacon sleep in on Sundays, but today he and Adam were officially moving in. The three of us already spent almost every night together, and we were tired of not having a bed and a space that was all of ours.

They were moving in with me, since I had the most space.

"Could you do that without the orgasmic groaning?" Paige asked as Adam walked toward the stairs. "Some of us are still working on our first cup of coffee."

Bryan snorted. "Speak for yourself. I've had plenty of coffee and I still don't want to hear it. They made you listen to gross sex noises? Really? I call child abuse."

"I can't help it if Deacon is a bear," Adam said.

Paige made a gagging motion. "In the morning."

"You meant to add *in the morning* to the end of that sentence," Bryan added.

Adam shrugged. "Did I? I don't think I did. *Rawr.*"

I just laughed. The four of them, my men and my twins, got along so well. It was wonderful to see, even if I wasn't quite comfortable with them vocalizing that specific topic.

Deacon was unusually bright-eyed when he and Adam joined us again.

When I mentioned it, Deacon gave me a quick kiss on the forehead. "Of course I am," he said. "Today's *the* day." His hair had grown back over the past year, and he had it pulled into a high ponytail. I had to admit, I loved the look, especially with those sexy, tattooed forearms on display.

Perfect reason to be all smiles, as far as I was concerned.

We spent the next several hours making trips between Deacon's shop and the house, transferring boxes and furniture.

Adam filmed a lot of it for his channel, which had exploded in popularity as he'd shifted to focus on weird and unique shops like Deacon's, Aubrey's, and Sebastian's. Adam included a little bit about his life— our lives—too, but I wasn't worried about him putting private information out in the world. He was cautious about how he shared.

He used his platform to promote little shops all over the country. A lot of them would send him video and he either compiled episodes from what they sent him, or flew out and spent a few days with them to get the footage he needed.

Deacon's shop still got more coverage than everyone else. Partly because Adam was biased, but Deacon's business had grown as well.

He did a lot of sales on a consignment basis, including making connections for other shops on the streets. He sold a lot of interesting antiques for people who didn't want to get into reselling but had things they wanted to get rid of.

Both Adam and Deacon were loving what they were doing, and I loved seeing them so happy.

We finished moving everything in, and ordered pizza.

As the five of us sat around eating, laughing, and just enjoying the day, I absorbed all of it. Not because I was worried it wouldn't last, but because I wanted to remember every bit of this amazing life going forward.

I wanted the twins to know this was their home still, even if they didn't live here anymore. They were welcome back any time, and their rooms would stay theirs.

We wrapped up, and it was time to take Paige to the airport. I didn't want her on such a late flight, but she insisted it was the best way to make sure she got to spend time with us and still make work in the morning.

"Before you go, I almost forgot." Deacon held up a finger, then jogged upstairs.

Paige and Bryan gave me a questioning look, and I shrugged. Whatever he was up to, it ought to be interesting.

Deacon was back a moment later, with a brown paper wrapped square. "For your apartment." He handed the picture to Paige.

"Ooh, present." She ripped into the wrapping without hesitation, her brother cringing the entire time. I assumed because she wasn't cutting everything away carefully.

Paige's jaw dropped when she saw what was inside, and I couldn't help my smile. It was a picture frame with two photos of her tank—the original image of the original owner, and a second one with her, Bryan, and Adam standing in front of the vehicle.

"I love it. Thank you." Paige threw her arms around Deacon's neck. She hugged Adam as well. "Because you took the picture."

I hated to tear her away from them, or send her on her way, but she had a flight to catch.

I took Paige to the airport and Bryan rode along. When we dropped her off at the curb, we exchanged a billion hugs and almost as many sniffles and tears. Even Bryan was swiping at his cheeks.

After we watched Paige walk into the airport, I took Bryan back to his apartment. I was so proud of my kids—all grown up and following their dreams.

I dropped him off as well and headed home. The home I'd bought so many years ago just needing a place for myself and my babies where I could hide from the world. The house I'd mourned in. Watched my children grow up in. And now the house I was starting the next chapter of my life in.

Adam and Deacon were there, waiting with kisses and love.

Everything that had happened in this home had made me, my children, the people we were now.

And I couldn't wait to see what came next, with my amazing guys and wonderful life.

———

THANK you for falling in love with Brooke, Deacon, and Adam.

The sweet sexiness continues for Carly in THE LAYOVER. Carly's happy with single life. When the sexy men she hooks up with during her layover turn out to be her new clients, she knows she should keep her distance. But 'just one more night' becomes another and another. She finds herself falling for both men, and losing her heart to their daughter. But when Carly's contract is up, she's going back home, and leaving this all behind.